"So you're saying dating me wouldn't be aboveboard?"

"First of all, we're not dating."

Grant tried to ignore the pang of disappointment Rebekah's words brought him despite the fact that he'd told himself the same thing the past several weeks. "Okay, obviously we're not dating. I think we both made it pretty clear that night that we weren't in the market for a serious relationship. However, with circumstances being what they are—" he managed a pointed look at her still-flat stomach behind the lap belt "—don't you think people are going to eventually find out that you're pregnant?"

Just then a loud yip sounded from somewhere in the back of the car. Grant and Rebekah nearly butted foreheads as they whipped their necks around quickly. A mangy animal with long, gray fur covering its eyes poked its head up from the storage area in the very rear of the car.

"What in the hell kind of animal is that?"

"I think it's that stray dog that everyone has been trying to catch."

* * *

FUREVER YOURS: Finding forever homes— and hearts!—has never been so easy

D0190997

Dear Reader,

I was so excited to participate in the first Furever Yours series stories for Harlequin Special Edition. I'm one of those people who gets teary-eyed every time I go to an animal shelter, so a story about a pet rescue makes me want to run out and adopt all the animals.

In *It Started with a Pregnancy*, secondary characters Bunny and Birdie Whitaker reminded me of our longtime family friend Patty. Patty loves dogs, cats, baby bunnies, wild birds, you name it. We joke that she provides her local veterinarian with so much business, they should name a wing after her.

But Patty doesn't stop with animals. She has the ability to make every single person with whom she interacts feel important. As a kid, I adored Patty so much, I even tried to dress like her, usually in a matching pink tracksuit and headband. Going to her house for our girls-only slumber parties always made me feel so special—even when Tootser, her crotchety schnauzer, constantly growled at me. I swear, Tootser had to be the meanest dog who ever lived and yet he was her baby.

But even dogs like Tootser need a home and their own Bunny/Birdie/Patty to love them. I'm hoping that *It Started with a Pregnancy*, as well as the first five books in the Furever Yours series, brings more awareness to all the wonderful animals out there looking for their forever homes.

For more information on my other Harlequin Special Edition books, visit my website at christyjeffries.com, or chat with me on Twitter, @christyjeffries. You can also find me on Facebook and Instagram. I'd love to hear from you.

Enjoy,

Christy Jeffries

Facebook.com/AuthorChristyJeffries

Instagram.com/Christy_Jeffries/

It Started with a Pregnancy

Christy Jeffries

Special thanks and acknowledgment to Christy Jeffries for her contribution to the Furever Yours continuity.

Recycling programs
for this product may
not exist in your area.

ISBN-13: 978-1-335-57391-9

It Started with a Pregnancy

Copyright © 2019 by Harlequin Books S.A.

Printed in U.S.A.

www.Harlequin.com

Christy Jeffries graduated from the University of California, Irvine, with a degree in criminology, and received her Juris Doctor from California Western School of Law. But drafting court documents and working in law enforcement was merely an apprenticeship for her current career in the dynamic field of mommyhood and romance writing. She lives in Southern California with her patient husband, two energetic sons and one sassy grandmother. Follow her online at christyjeffries.com.

Books by Christy Jeffries

Harlequin Special Edition

Sugar Falls, Idaho

A Marine for His Mom
Waking Up Wed
From Dare to Due Date
The Matchmaking Twins
The Makeover Prescription
A Family Under the Stars
The Firefighter's Christmas Reunion
The SEAL's Secret Daughter

American Heroes

A Proposal for the Officer

Montana Mavericks

The Maverick's Bridal Bargain

Montana Mavericks: The Lonelyhearts Ranch

The Maverick's Christmas to Remember

Visit the Author Profile page at Harlequin.com.

To Patty Kawano Barberio. Thank you for taking a young and sometimes smart-mouthed girl under your wing and being a bonus role model. You showed me how to shop for jewelry, how to play blackjack, how to travel independently and how to love dogs again. Most importantly, you showed me how to be kind to others. You are the heart of my hearts.

Chapter One

Rebekah Taylor stared at the pregnancy test in her hand. How could it be positive? They'd used protection, one of the condoms she'd gotten as a gag gift from a friend's bachelorette party a couple of years ago. Sure, the thing had been an embarrassing shade of glittery pink, but it should have worked in the heat of the moment.

Except it hadn't.

Had the condom expired? Rebekah glanced at the reflection of her wide, panic-filled eyes in the mirrored medicine cabinet. Every six months she methodically went through all her kitchen and bathroom cupboards and threw out everything that was even close to its expiration date.

How had she missed something as important as this? Sighing, she slouched lower on the toilet seat. Probably because she'd hidden the little heart-shaped box in a back corner of her nightstand drawer, where it was out of sight and out of mind. It probably would've stayed in its hiding spot indefinitely if she hadn't been so desperate.

And so lonely.

Although, at least she'd had a condom to start with, unlike the carefree Grant Whitaker, who'd come to her house unprepared for a one-night stand eight weeks ago. Not that either one of them had been expecting things to get physical that night.

In fact, Rebekah hadn't been able to stand the guy the first few times he'd visited Spring Forest, North Carolina. Flying in from Florida in his board shorts and T-shirts and flip-flops every couple of months, he looked more like a surf instructor than any kind of business professional.

And the weird thing was, for such a relaxed-looking guy, he'd always watched Rebekah like a hawk. She was the director of Furever Paws, his elderly aunts' nonprofit organization, yet he constantly kept his eye on her—as though he expected she would stuff her pockets full of dog biscuits and sneak them into the puppy kennels if his back was turned. Of course, he was pretty much like that with everyone who worked at the shelter. Everyone who wasn't family, at least. The guy was undoubtedly protective of his relatives.

"Nobody would mistake you for being a part of the Whitaker family," she told her reflection. As a biracial woman with an African American mother and an Irish American father, Rebekah's deep bronze skin and black, springy curls were a stark contrast to Grant's lighter, sun-kissed complexion and wavy blond hair. Would their baby favor one of them over the other? Or would their child be blessed with the best of both gene sets. "Stop it!" she commanded herself. She'd barely known about the pregnancy for three minutes and already she was letting her emotions overrule her logic.

Maybe that first test was just a dud. Rebekah frantically tore open another package, this time from the manufacturer that promised a plus sign instead of two striped lines. Ten minutes later, though, the result was the same.

She would've sunk to her knees right there in her brand-new townhome and curled herself into a little ball if she'd thought it would help. But grown women with mortgages and MBAs and lead positions at nonprofits didn't break down and cry every time something went wrong.

They examined the problem, researched solutions and made lists of what to do next. Taking out a pad of paper she wrote down, *1. Make doctor appointment.* She got as far as writing the number *2* on her to-do list, but then couldn't think of what she should do next.

Tell Grant?

A tremor shook through her at the thought of how that conversation might go. The man would probably react in one of two ways. He might say, "Right on," and then eventually forget about her and their kid because they didn't fit with his bachelor lifestyle. Or he might accuse her of getting pregnant on purpose to trap him— just like Trey once had.

There really wasn't any sense in doing anything until she'd confirmed things with the doctor. Crumpling the list in her hand, she tossed it into the wastebasket, right on top of the pink-and-blue boxes.

Walking to the kitchen, she flipped on her coffee machine out of habit before remembering that pregnant women were supposed to limit their caffeine intake. A tic started at her temple and Rebekah wondered how she could possibly give up coffee for nine whole months.

Wait. Longer if she decided to breastfeed.

Her cell phone pinged behind her and she turned and swiped the screen, looking at the text message her mom had just sent.

Did we book my class's field trip for the first or second Tuesday of September?

Rebekah pinched the bridge of her nose. Her mother was a first-grade teacher and had been begging Rebekah to set up a tour of the pet rescue for a bunch of six-year-olds. Thank goodness she didn't have to deal with that headache today.

Mom, it's scheduled for the eighth. I put it in the online calendar I set up for you last week.

Dimples, you know I'm never going to use that calendar thingy. It's too complicated. Plus, your dad accidentally deleted the app off my phone when he was trying to reset our wi-fi password.

Before Rebekah could respond, another message popped up on her screen. This time from her dad.

Hey there, Dimples. Your mom screwed up our wi-fi password again and I can't find the paper where you wrote down all our log-in codes. Any chance you can come up this weekend and reset things for us?

Rebekah was convinced that her parents purposely remained technologically challenged because it gave them the perfect excuse to summon their dutiful daughter home for long weekend visits. Normally, she didn't mind the thirty-minute trips to Raleigh, but Rebekah wasn't quite ready to face them yet.

After typing a detailed response to her father, including a description of where she'd filed their log-in information and an online link to a video giving them a step-by-step tutorial on how to change their password, Rebekah found the number for a local obstetrician with excellent ratings and took a deep breath before placing her call.

A male receptionist answered and Rebekah had to clear her throat several times before finally getting the words out. "I think I might be pregnant and I'd like to schedule an appointment with Dr. Singh."

"Congratulations," the deep masculine voice replied and Rebekah took solace in the fact that at least there was one man in this world who was happy about her revelation. "How far along are you?"

"Um, I'm thinking eight weeks," she offered, going off the app on her phone that tracked her cycle. She could organize everything else in her life to a T, but much to her frustration, she'd never been very regular when it came to her periods.

"And do you know the date of conception?"

Embarrassment threaded through the lower half of her torso, squeezing around her stomach. Of course she knew the exact date of conception. She even remembered the spicy lettuce wraps and the blackberry mojitos that had been on special during that fateful happy hour. It had only been one night of weakness. Yet apparently, one night was all it took. Instead of admitting as much to the receptionist, she simply told him the date.

"Usually Dr. Singh doesn't see her patients until they're closer to twelve weeks. I can put you on the books for October."

Rebekah clenched her jaw so tightly, her back molars vibrated. It was currently the end of August and there was no way she could wait that long without knowing for sure. She hated to even think about the last time she'd found herself in a similar situation, let alone use it as an excuse to garner special treatment. However, she needed to take action, she needed to be in control of the situation this time. "Actually, I have a history of ectopic pregnancy, so I'm sure the doctor will want to see me sooner."

"Of course," he replied, and she heard him tapping on a keyboard. "In that case, the soonest we can get you in will be next Thursday."

He listed the appointment openings, and after finding one that worked for her schedule, Rebekah wrote down the time in her day planner. Then she mumbled her thanks and disconnected the call so she could also program the appointment into the calendar app on her smartphone.

Getting into the shower, she made a firm decision to put the whole thing out of her mind until next week.

That vow lasted a whole forty-five minutes—when her teal blue Fiat was idling at the intersection near a large chain drugstore. She glanced at the clock on her dashboard and wasn't surprised to see she had plenty of time to swing inside, grab some prenatal vitamins and still get to work half an hour early.

When she came out of the pharmacy, she walked over to Great American Bakery, because she couldn't very well take the vitamin on an empty stomach. Besides, if she couldn't have coffee, then a warm chocolate croissant would be the next best thing to settle her nerves. No, not her nerves. She refused to be nervous. This uneasy feeling in her tummy was simply due to hunger. Or the pregnancy cravings she'd only heard about but never experienced.

Climbing back into her car, she realized that she'd surely get crumbs and chocolate all over her brand-new silk blouse. Many of the people employed at Furever Paws wore much more functional clothes for working with animals, but Rebekah had a lunch with a potential donor this afternoon and then a city council meeting tonight. Her bosses, Bunny and Birdie Whitaker, were going to request a zoning ordinance to allow for a cell tower on their farm, which adjoined the pet rescue's learning center. The tower would provide the sisters some much-needed financial revenue, and it would provide the town's new development of Kingdom Creek some better wireless service.

Not everyone in the suburban town was happy with how quickly their little city was blossoming, though, so she was expecting to confront some annoyed townspeople tonight.

By the time she pulled into her parking spot at work, her stomach was growling and her temples were pounding from the beginnings of a headache—probably due to a lack of caffeine. Grabbing the bags containing the vitamins and the croissant, she tried to shove both in her already full tote.

It wasn't like her to pick up a breakfast treat and not bring in a box to share with everyone else at work. However, she didn't necessarily feel very social this morning and just wanted to sneak into her private office and hide behind a mountain of paperwork and a closed door.

Many of Rebekah's coworkers were more focused on the rescue center's animals than on the humans who worked there. So hopefully nobody would notice that her entire world was threatening to topple off its axis. She checked her reflection in the rearview mirror, assuring herself that there was no sign of a pregnancy glow or anything else that might give away her secret before she was ready to disclose it.

Thankfully, it would be easy enough to avoid Grant until she was able to confirm that her pregnancy was real—and had worked out the best way to tell him. She'd already managed to avoid him since their night together, although it helped that he lived in another state. The last contact she'd had from him was the note with his cell number that he'd left the morning he sneaked out of her townhouse.

Not wanting the temptation, she'd immediately thrown the number away without programming it into her own phone. As amazing as he'd made her feel that night, there was no way she could allow a repeat performance of their one-night stand. And even now, there still might not be a reason for her to call him. Her pregnancy wasn't confirmed yet—not officially. Her father had made his career on giving people advice and was especially fond of the phrase, *Don't borrow tomorrow's problems today.* Rebekah repeated those words in her mind.

Balancing her purse and tote bag on one shoulder, Rebekah grabbed her other two bags and used the thick wedge heel of her espadrille sandal to close the car door behind her.

She took a deep breath before heading toward the entrance and then froze at the sound of the unmistakable deep voice coming from behind her. "Looks like the early bird definitely gets the worm all to himself this morning."

Grant Whitaker was unfolding his long, athletic frame from some nondescript rental car she hadn't even noticed in the parking lot. Right this second, he didn't look so much like an early bird as he did a hawk. Wait. That meant that she would be the worm in this scenario. Although, she couldn't deny that she was currently trying to slink on by without drawing his deep blue gaze and giving herself away.

The second he gave her that knowing smile, though,

her mouth went dry and her tummy went completely topsy-turvy.

Or maybe that feeling was actually her first bout of morning sickness.

Grant Whitaker's elderly aunts, Birdie and Bunny, loved it whenever he found the time to fly in from Jacksonville to visit them and help out at Furever Paws. Apparently, though, they had kept the details of this visit to themselves. Judging by Rebekah Taylor's wide-eyed stare and dropped jaw, she had no clue that his aunts had asked him to review the latest marketing plans in order to get more people at their adoption events.

Even if his aunts hadn't asked for his help, he probably would've found another reason to get back to Spring Forest to see Rebekah before long. He hadn't talked to the no-nonsense director of the animal shelter in more than a month. He'd thought they'd finally turned a corner after sharing a couple of drinks—and much more—that night. She'd been sound asleep when he'd had to leave to catch his flight back to Florida, so he'd left his number in a place where he knew she wouldn't miss it. And while he hadn't expected a call the first few days after they'd spent the night together, Grant had been hoping for at least a "see you next time you're in town" text.

Rebekah Taylor was as straitlaced as they came and had a reputation around the pet shelter for running a tight ship. Or as tight a ship as one could run with the elderly Whitaker sisters in charge. The director was wound so tightly, she reminded Grant of one of those coils that launched like a bouncing spring the second someone released some of the pressure. Several weeks ago, when he'd run into her and her friends at happy hour, he'd ended up being the lucky one who'd helped her unwind.

He'd had a good time that night—better than good, if he was being honest with himself—and he'd thought she'd enjoyed herself, as well. In fact, right this second, his fingers twitched instinctively, as if they were also remembering the way her muscles had clenched against them when he'd brought her to...

Grant's already sunburned neck grew warm and he had to give his head a quick shake to clear it while Rebekah fumbled with her keys as she tried to unlock the front door.

"Here, can I give you a hand?" he asked as he reached out to take the keys from her. The second his thumb grazed her palm, an electrical current shot through him. As she jerked her arm back, he realized that she must've felt it, too.

So the attraction was definitely still there, even if Rebekah was holding her giant tote bag between them like a shield, blocking his view of her full, round breasts. As though he hadn't already committed to memory the sight of the dark bronze skin framing deep-brown nipples.

She had a death grip on the two white bags in her other hand and blew a curly strand of black hair out of her face. While she didn't look angry, she also didn't look very pleased to see him. In fact, the smooth skin at the base of her neck revealed a jumping pulse, making him think the overly controlling office director wasn't feeling all that in control right this second.

Grant tried to hide his grin at this sudden revelation. Just because she'd let her guard down around him once didn't mean she'd be willing to do it again. Rebekah was a tough woman to read, but he remembered her slightly tipsy words that night as she'd finished her third mojito after her friends left the bar. "We can't let anyone know about us drinking together like this. It would be extremely unprofessional for me to socialize with a member of my bosses' family."

"Then we probably shouldn't tell anyone that I'm going to come over to your place when we leave the bar," he'd replied just before signaling for the check. Her thick lashes had lowered seductively and one corner of her full lips had lifted in invitation. It'd been a bold pickup line from a guy who normally didn't have to resort to lines to get women, and Grant hadn't expected it to work with someone as reserved as Rebekah. It turned out that his taking charge that night had worked out extremely well for both of them.

However, something in her hazel eyes—possibly panic—told Grant that he shouldn't re-create the same take-charge strategy at her workplace. Or in the light of day. He cleared his throat and turned back to the door, jamming the first key he saw into the lock. It only went halfway.

"It's the third one," she said, using her chin to nod toward the key ring that had suddenly become slippery in his damp hands. It took another two tries, and when he finally pulled the glass door open, she rushed by him in a cloud of the plumeria scent she always wore—he'd noticed the bottle of expensive lotion on her bathroom counter that night—and headed straight past the empty reception desk and down the hallway leading toward the business offices.

Grant stood there for a few seconds, letting the air-conditioning from inside filter past him to the humid summer heat outside. She hadn't even thanked him for getting the door, let alone said goodbye. It was one thing to want to keep their personal business on the down low, it was another to completely brush him off. Some of the animal handlers were probably on duty in the back, but since the shelter wouldn't be open to the public until ten o'clock, there wasn't anyone in the newly refinished reception area to see them. It was almost as though she wanted to pretend he wasn't even there.

Grant wasn't in the habit of having one-night stands with his aunts' employees—or anyone else, for that matter—so a part of him understood her desire to try to forget the whole thing had ever happened. He'd felt the same way the past few weeks when it had become apparent that she wasn't going to call him. By avoiding any sort of conversation, Rebekah was actually providing him with the perfect escape, the perfect excuse to avoid any sort of messy emotions or awkward conversations about how things could never work between them.

But the memory of Rebekah's curves pressed against him and the sound of her throaty moans were too fresh in his mind.

Plus, he still had her keys.

Grant's flip-flops slapped against the lacquered finish of the concrete floor as he took long strides toward the biggest office. The door was already closed so he gave a brisk knock before twisting the handle and letting himself inside.

Rebekah stood behind her desk, both hands braced on the tidy surface and her chest puffed out, as though she'd been in the middle of some deep breathing exercise before he'd barged in.

Grant didn't do tension or uncomfortable silences. So when his eyes landed on one of the bags in front of her, he shifted gears to a neutral topic.

"Sutter's Pharmacy, huh?" He hooked his thumbs into the waistband of his favorite board shorts and tried to appear as casual as possible. "Are you feeling out of sorts?"

"I'm fine!" Rebekah's words came out in a squeak and her round eyes grew even larger as they filled with alarm. Whoa. He'd just been trying to lighten the mood. He hadn't meant to make her uncomfortable.

"If you say so. Anyway, I came in here because you forgot your keys," he said, dangling them in front of his chest. His father had raised him to be a gentleman and he knew the proper thing to do would be to place the key ring with the silver softball charm on her desk. But he couldn't stop himself from testing to see if the sensation he'd felt from their earlier physical contact had just been a fluke.

Rebekah was a tall woman and easily reached one arm across her desk. When her fingers met his, another flare of heat shot through him. She yanked her hand back so quickly, it knocked one of the white sacks off her tote bag.

There was a rattling sound as something rolled out of the bag and fell to the floor right by his feet.

Rebekah must've raced around the desk because she was suddenly diving at the container in front of him. But she wasn't fast enough. The words on the label flashed in his brain as though they were blinking in neon lights, even after she clutched the bottle to her chest.

Something in his gut twisted, and the air in his lungs suspended. It took him several times to get the words out and his voice sounded far way when he finally asked, "Why are you taking prenatal vitamins?"

Chapter Two

Rebekah bit her lip, trying to resist the urge to hide the bottle behind her back. She'd already flung herself on the ground in front of him as though she were a combat soldier jumping onto a live grenade. At this point, there was no way to pretend the emotional explosion hadn't already detonated around them.

Still.

How had he read the label so quickly?

She didn't realize she'd spoken the question out loud until Grant replied, "I won the national speed-reading championships for my high school four years in a row."

"You're a speed reader?" she asked as she rose to her feet, seizing on the opportunity to redirect the conversation.

"I was also the Duval County Spelling Bee champion

in eighth grade," he added. "But I don't especially feel a need to discuss my academic accomplishments right this second. Is there something you want to tell me, Rebekah?"

She watched his soft lips move, yet his question sounded so formal, as did the way he said her name. Her parents were the only ones who called her Dimples, and she hated it when people used the common nicknames Becky or Bekah, or even Beck. So it wasn't as though Grant should be calling her anything other than Rebekah. Still, his question felt like a chastisement all the same.

Straightening her spine, she forced herself to look him directly in those ocean-blue eyes and said, "I might be pregnant."

"Whoa." He sank into the paisley upholstered chair right in front of her, swiping the sun-bleached blond hair off his forehead. "I mean…whoa."

Yep, *that* was the response she'd been anticipating.

And now that he was acting as she'd initially expected, Rebekah felt her own role fall back into place as she took charge of the situation. "I took a test this morning, but I'm waiting for the doctor to confirm it."

"How…" he started, then scrubbed a hand over the golden stubble on his jaw. "I mean…"

"How did this happen?" she offered. "I'm sure the usual way."

"I was actually going to ask how far along you are." He used his tan forearms to push himself up a little straighter and Rebekah wondered if he was already calculating the date in his mind.

"I'm four weeks late, so that would put me at eight weeks." She held up a warning finger. "*If* I am, in fact, pregnant. Like I said, there's no need to get all worked up over a store-bought test."

Or two tests, if anyone was counting.

Grant sucked in a deep breath, his nostrils flaring slightly as he exhaled. "So when do we go to the doctor to confirm it?"

We. The skin on the back of her neck tingled. "Well, *I* have an appointment next week. If you want, I can send you a text afterward and let you know if there's any news."

There was no point in mentioning that she'd need to ask for his cell phone number again.

"A text? If there's any news?" When his eyes finally focused on hers, Rebekah swallowed a tiny lump of guilt. There was accusation practically shooting from their blue depths. "Were you even planning to tell me?"

"Of course I planned to tell you." Eventually. After she'd figured out what she was going to do. She twisted her lower lip between her teeth.

She waited for the next question to come—the one about whether the baby was his—but he only studied her intently before slowly nodding.

Grant slid his smartphone out of his pocket and she remembered when the device had been sitting out on the table that evening while they were closing down happy hour. She'd commented on the battered cover and the cracked screen and he'd told her the story of how he'd been testing out one of his company's waterproof cases when he'd wiped out near a coral reef and cracked his surfboard in half. The still-functional phone was one of his biggest marketing tools when it came to selling his company's tech products. Not that she had a very clear picture of exactly what it was he did for the company.

This wasn't good, she thought, giving her head a quick shake to clear it. She might be having this man's baby, yet she didn't even know what he did for a living.

"What day is the appointment?" he asked as he swiped at an app on his phone. It was the same online calendar she'd unsuccessfully tried to get her parents to use.

"Um…" Rebekah tilted her head, unsure if she wanted him to know. Unfortunately, he'd practically accused her of keeping the pregnancy from him already and she didn't want to give him any reason to think that she had something to hide. Besides, it wasn't like he'd actually stay in town long enough to go with her. Or that he'd even want to go. "It's next Thursday."

"Uh-huh," he said as he tapped something else. "What time?"

"Grant, you aren't actually planning to go to the doctor's office with me, are you?"

At this, he lifted his eyes to hers again and she could see that the full force of his earlier suspicion had returned. "Of course I'm planning to be there. You didn't think I'd leave you to go through this alone, did you?"

There was no polite way to answer that question. Frankly, there wasn't even an honest way of answering without admitting that not only had she been thinking that exact thing, she was hoping for it. Instead, she opted to remind him of the logistics involved. "But don't you have to be back in Jacksonville for work or…something?"

His fingers flew over his cracked phone screen, typing as he spoke. "Actually, I'm flying to a digital marketing conference in San Francisco tonight after I check in on my aunts. I'll just change my return flight so I can swing by here on the way home next week."

Rebekah heard him speaking, but the only word her brain seized on was *aunts*. A rush of unease shot to her stomach. "You can't tell your aunts about this."

"About what?" he asked, his attention seemingly focused fully on the electronic device in his hands and—luckily—not on the beads of sweat breaking out across Rebekah's forehead. She resisted the urge to grab one of the vet reports off her desk and fan her heated face.

"About me. About us." Her finger pointed back and forth at each of them, before her hand dropped to her still-flat belly. "And especially not about the baby."

He lifted his head finally, his eyes zeroing in on her. Not in the suspicious way that she was accustomed to from him, but in a sexy, hungry sort of way. All that tension in her tummy doubled and a sudden warmth spread under her skin.

Lord help her, but even as she faced the very man who now had the power to redirect her entire future, she was still hopelessly attracted to him.

Stiffening her shoulders, Rebekah commanded her body to get itself together. This reaction must be some sort of pregnancy-induced hormonal imbalance.

Not that she was exactly mother material herself, but Grant was the complete opposite of the type of guy she would choose to father her baby. What made things even more unbearable was the way his elderly aunts doted on him and acted as if he'd hung the moon, making his job down in Jacksonville sound like the most important career in the world. In reality, he worked for a tech company that encouraged beach days and flexible hours and spontaneous yoga sessions in their cubicle-free environment. While some might describe him as easygoing and charming, to Rebekah, Grant seemed like one of those men who'd never really grown up. Maybe it was because she'd yet to see him dressed in a shirt with a collar.

Or a shirt that didn't highlight his strong, broad shoulders.

As she stared at the faded logo on the soft cotton tee stretched across his muscular chest, she ignored the desire curling inside her and wondered for the hundredth time this morning how she'd ended up in this situation with this man, of all people.

Because he was sexy as hell. That's how.

"Rebekah." Grant finally rose to his feet before walking over to stand in front of her. When she ducked her head to avoid those piercing eyes, he softly placed a finger under her chin and lifted her face to meet his gaze. "I won't say a word to anyone until we get the green light from the doctor."

All she could manage was a slight nod and a slow release of air from her too-tight lungs. She didn't want to talk about green lights or anything else with him until she had a concrete plan in place.

A plan that most likely wouldn't involve her spending any more time with Grant Whitaker.

Standing face-to-face, Grant didn't immediately remove his hand from the curve of Rebekah's cheek as he studied her resigned expression.

It wasn't that he didn't trust her. Despite the fact that he doubted she would've told him about the pregnancy quite so soon if she hadn't nervously knocked over that bag, he did believe she was honest and honorable. But there was something about the woman that always threw him off-balance. Something that she kept locked up tight behind the professional clothes and the detailed financial reports and the organized meeting notes she always passed off to his aunts, who would inadvertently leave the meticulously typed documents behind in the kennel of a sick Labrador or under a pallet of kitty-litter bags. In fact, while he'd been waiting for Rebekah in the parking lot this morning, he'd wandered over to the stables and found one of the llamas eating the cell tower proposal that Rebekah had drafted for a city council meeting.

Rebekah was nothing if not thorough. Which made it difficult for him to believe that she hadn't already formulated a specific course of action.

Eventually, she took a step back, forcing his hand to drop as she pivoted to rearrange some papers on her desk. Without making eye contact, she began to speak. "Well, I appreciate you stopping by and…you know…"

"Bringing you your keys?" he suggested, not about to let her simply dismiss him without some sort of confirmation that she would be in contact with him soon. "Oh, and for offering my unflagging support at the doctor's appointment as well as with any decisions that need to be made?"

"Are you hoping for a certain decision, Grant?" Even from this side view, he could see her shoulders square off as though she was preparing for battle. So it was no surprise when she fully faced him with the dimples in her cheeks completely hidden as she forced out a heavy breath. "Perhaps one that lets you off the hook?"

For the first time in his life, he felt completely un-equipped to handle the situation before him. Grant was the problem solver in his family, the one who dropped everything to help those who needed him. However, the determined line of Rebekah's clenched jaw suggested that she didn't want his assistance in solving this problem.

Not that her being pregnant was a problem, he corrected himself as he rolled his shoulders backward to loosen the tense muscles.

He carefully thought about his next words. "Actually, if the decision were up to me, I'd have a house full of kids."

Her perfectly arched brows shot nearly to her hairline, and before she could open her mouth, he already knew what she was thinking.

"Not that I would have purposely gotten you pregnant!" The words tumbled out of his mouth defensively and his right hand lifted as though he were swearing a solemn oath.

"Shhh!" Her eyes darted right past him and toward the reception desk. From outside the office, he could hear a door opening and what sounded like a couple of volunteers discussing last night's episode of *Top Chef*.

He lowered his voice. "I'm just stating for the record that none of this was my intent. In fact, I even used that hot-pink condom that left glitter all over my..."

She immediately clapped her hand to his mouth.

He mumbled more words behind her palm, but she didn't remove it. So he did what any man would do when presented with a beautiful woman's skin so close to his lips. He kissed the sensitive spot right between her thumb and forefinger.

Rebekah yanked her palm back and her eyes narrowed into a warning glance. Her voice came out in a fierce whisper. "Well, at least *I* had…protection."

Her implication hung in the air between them.

"Listen, I'm sorry for not being better prepared." It was an odd feeling, being on the defensive like this, and for a moment it was difficult for him to get the words out. "As much as you might want to think otherwise, I usually don't go home with—"

"Grant," Aunt Bunny interrupted as she swept into the office. Rebekah jumped away from him so quickly, he heard a *thunk* against her desk. The sweet older woman glanced down at his preferred beach attire. "I wasn't expecting you this early. Were the waves too small to hold your interest this morning?"

"You know me too well, Aunt Bunny." Grant lifted his arms and shrugged his shoulders. "When I saw that the surf was under two feet, I caught an earlier flight into Raleigh–Durham and figured I'd rent a car and swing by to go over the marketing plans for the upcoming adoption events."

Bunny's attention turned to Rebekah, who was holding herself so rigidly she could've been one of his surfboards. Except with many more curves. Did it make him a bad person to want to pull the sexy and stiff woman close to him and run his hands along her waist and over her full hips until she relaxed and melted in his arms?

His normally absentminded aunt might tend to pay

more attention to animals of the four-legged variety than she did to humans, but her eyes were uncharacteristically sharp as her glance bounced back and forth between Grant and Rebekah. Finally, Bunny asked, "Where are they?"

"Where are what?" Grant sidestepped around the upholstered chair, pivoting his body in the hopes of blocking Bunny's view of the empty pharmacy bag threatening to fall off Rebekah's desk again. He had to command his own eyes not to scan the room for the prenatal vitamins.

"Your marketing plans?" His aunt lifted a thin gray brow.

"Oh. On my laptop," Grant replied, hoping she wouldn't ask why he'd left his computer in the rental car. He didn't want to admit that he'd been in such a hurry to follow Rebekah inside the building this morning, he hadn't given his initial excuse for flying into town a second thought.

"All that will have to wait." Bunny waved a work-roughened hand at him. "Since I have both of you together, come outside and see our new sign. The old one was destroyed with all that tornado damage, and we wanted to install an extra one at the edge of the parking lot so people can now see it from the road."

"Oh, they're early." Rebekah jumped at the excuse to get out of the office and away from the conversation they'd been having. Literally. Her knee-length skirt fluttered open at the slit as she made a little hop to skip past him.

As he followed her and Bunny past the reception

desk and through the lobby, Grant had to restrain himself from hurrying to catch up with them. Now that Rebekah was no longer watching him so intently, waiting to see if he'd give the wrong reaction, he could take a moment to let her words sink in.

She was possibly pregnant. With his child.

What he'd told her about wanting a house full of children was true. However, he hadn't expected to become a father quite so soon. Rebekah's earlier revelation had landed like a sucker punch to the gut. The blow had been swift and unexpected and heavy, dropping him into the chair as he attempted to wrap his mind around what had just happened. Then, just as quickly, Rebekah had pulled back emotionally, that initial hit leaving a hollow, empty feeling in his stomach.

He was used to being needed and usually relished his role as the guy who came in and solved things. It was what made him so good at his job. It was why his mom and his sisters often relied on him to keep his family's surf shop on top of the latest trends. It was why he was currently in Spring Forest to oversee his elderly aunts' troubled financial situation.

But Rebekah didn't seem to want *anything* from him. At least, not yet. Maybe she would change her mind after the appointment next week.

Either way, the woman would need to get used to Grant being around. If she was, in fact, having his child, she would soon learn that he always put his family first.

Chapter Three

Rebekah had never been so relieved to see someone as when Bunny Whitaker had walked into her office five minutes ago. Sure, she'd had to paste a calm smile on her face while awkwardly reaching behind her blindly in order to shove the bottle of prenatal vitamins into the tote bag sitting on top of her desk.

Still, the older woman's fortunate arrival got Rebekah away from facing more of Grant's potential follow-up questions. Questions Rebekah didn't have all the answers for yet.

Speaking of the man, his flip-flops smacked against the flat gravel as he caught up with them in the parking lot. Rebekah's jaw clenched as he approached behind her. She had to swallow several times and take deep breaths in through her nose—not so much from annoyance at the man for always appearing at the worst times, but from the fact that her stomach was still doing somersaults and she was afraid that the morning-sickness fairy was currently paying her a visit.

"Hey, Aunt Bunny, what happened to the logo that my graphic designer sent you?" Grant asked from behind Rebekah's shoulder. Rebekah's eyes shot to the five-foot piece of painted aluminum tilted between two men wearing Signs 4 Less T-shirts.

Oh, no. Rebekah ignored the tiny rocks flicking between her toes and the soles of her wedge sandals as she strode across the parking lot to make sure she wasn't reading the sign wrong. She could hear her boss's voice as Bunny and Grant caught up to her.

"Well, the owner of Signs 4 Less felt real bad about not taking our advice to get his dog spayed, so when we found foster homes for all of her puppies, he offered to give us a great price if we just used standard lettering with no artwork."

"But I'd already negotiated a deal with the sign company out of Raleigh," Rebekah said. "I left the contract on your desk last week so you could approve it and sign it."

"I know, honey, but poor Marv had really bonded with those sweet pups and he was just an absolute wreck when he had to say goodbye to them. He started crying right there in the foster intake area and told me that his wife was moving out and his company wasn't doing so hot." Bunny shrugged her shoulders. "Plus, he gave us a nice discount if we cut out the logo and used fewer letters. I meant to tell you, but it must've slipped my mind."

Rebekah knew the woman and her sister were incredibly smart when it came to animal care, but when it came to business matters, they tended to follow their hearts instead of their heads. It was why they'd hired a director in the first place. It was also why they'd hired an attorney earlier this year to look into quite a bit of money that had gone missing. Unfortunately, they didn't always follow Rebekah's or the attorney's recommendations.

Worse than that, they tended to rely on the wrong people. They'd entrusted their money to their brother Gator—Grant's uncle—and it looked like he might have embezzled from them. And they'd entrusted this sign to Marv and…well…

Rebekah shot a pleading look at Grant and once she caught his attention, she pointed her chin first at the sign and then at his aunt. She wanted to tell him that this wasn't her fault, but first she needed to make sure he was seeing the same thing she was.

"Poor Marv, huh?" Grant nodded toward the sign that the workers were trying to hang between the wooden posts. "Let's just hope his return policy is better than his screen-printing skills."

In bright red letters were the words F-EVER PAWS, however the hyphen between the F and the E was so minuscule, that from far away it appeared to say, FEVER PAWS.

"I'm not sure if he has a return policy." Bunny pushed a strand of white hair back into her messy bun. "I think we should just leave it for a few days. I'm sure it'll grow on us."

Grant groaned and Rebekah experienced an unfamiliar tug of solidarity at his frustration. "Aunt Bunny, it says Fever Paws. Customers are going to think all the animals here are sick."

"Grant, we don't have *customers*." Bunny waved another hand at him. "We have prospective adopters looking for family companions."

"Well, your prospective adopters are going to drive right by when they see that sign," Grant replied.

"I guess you're right." His aunt sighed. "Well, we'll just have to call it a loss. I don't want Marv to be out any expense."

"Aunt Bunny." Grant gently rested his hand on the older woman's shoulder. "Your heart is bigger than your current bank account. The shelter really can't afford to take a loss like this. I'm going to tell the guys to take the sign back and re-do it."

Rebekah's heart softened at the way he gently, yet effectively steered his aunt back to reality. Really, it was *her* job to keep Furever Paws on a budget and, as the director, she should've been the one talking to the Signs 4 Less guys, not Grant. But she had plenty of other headaches to look forward to today, and if it got the man out of her hair for a few more minutes, she'd take whatever breaks she could get at this point.

Turning on her heel, she headed toward the shelter's entrance and thought about the cool air-conditioning and chocolate croissant waiting for her in her office. But a movement in the oak trees near the street caught her eye.

Bunny must've seen the streak of gray fur, too, because her boss let out a squeak before announcing, "Everyone stay completely still."

Rebekah knew that most of the staff at the shelter, as well as a few people in downtown Spring Forest, had reported sightings of the elusive gray dog that always seemed to outsmart them. She held her breath as Bunny slowly walked toward the stray, one of the treats she always carried in the front pocket of her faded overalls now outstretched in the palm of her hand.

Unfortunately, before Bunny could get within ten feet of the animal, one of the installation guys dropped his end of the FEVER PAWS sign and the sound of the aluminum clanking against the gravel burst out with a gong-like echo. The scruffy dog took off on its short legs, running directly toward the oncoming cars traveling in both directions on Little Creek Road.

Without looking, Bunny took off after the creature and only stopped when the horn of a big rig blasted through the air seconds before its huge chrome bumper nearly clipped the older woman. Grant caught up to his aunt first, and when Rebekah made it to the shoulder of the road, she could hear his admonishment about Bunny getting herself killed. His words fell on deaf ears as the woman craned her neck, watching the dog dart into the copse of trees on the other side of the street.

"I can't believe he got away again." Bunny shook her head as a mail delivery truck drove past, leaving a heavy gust of wind in its wake.

"Come on, Aunt Bunny," Grant said as he led his aunt toward the building. "If that dog wants to be caught, he'll come back."

"What do you mean *if* it wants to be caught? He's a stray, running from place to place. Why wouldn't he want a real home?" Rebekah heard the words coming out of her mouth and tried not to flinch at her accusatory tone.

Grant shrugged. "I mean not every animal should be domesticated. Some things are meant to be wild and untamed."

Some things? Or some *people*? Rebekah bit the inside of her cheek to keep from asking Grant if he was referring to himself. He'd better not be implying that her getting pregnant was any sort of attempt to domesticate him. Not that she'd ever want to, but even if she'd been willing to try, she knew she'd have better luck taming a tidal wave than taming the unpredictable force that was Grant Whitaker.

She took several calming breaths and commanded her legs to walk confidently back inside the building despite the tiny pieces of gravel that were now digging into the arches of her feet.

She refused to give him a second glance as she stormed ahead of him. The man had absolutely nothing to worry about. She wasn't about to force anyone to be anything they weren't.

The following Thursday, Grant was still kicking himself for not getting the address of Rebekah's doctor before he drove into Spring Forest. He'd had to take a red-eye flight from San Francisco with a layover in Chicago to make it to Raleigh before ten this morning. After landing, he'd barely had time to splash some water on his face and brush his teeth in the airport bathroom before racing to Furever Paws. If she'd called him, or offered her own phone number, he could've driven straight to the appointment and met her there with nobody being the wiser.

As it stood, they now risked having his aunts and everyone who worked at the shelter see them leave together. But at least he was pretty sure she'd be spending the morning at work since she'd scheduled the doctor's appointment during her lunch hour.

Grant checked the clock on the dash of his rental car right before pulling into the parking lot at the animal shelter, then felt his chest ease the second he spied Rebekah's blue car. She hadn't left yet.

Just as he turned off the engine, one of the double glass doors opened and a very beautiful Rebekah strode out wearing a sleeveless dress that hugged her waist before floating down to her knees. Again, she was wearing heels and the sight of her long, shapely legs made his lungs constrict.

By the time he'd exited his rental, she already had the back of her sporty little European car open and was wrestling the giant tote bag she always carried off her shoulder.

There were several other vehicles in the lot, but nobody else was outside. Still, Grant kept his voice low when he strode over to her. "Hey, looks like I'm just in time."

Rebekah jumped back, hitting her head on the corner of the rear hatch. Grant winced at the impact and sympathetically reached out to cradle her scalp in his palm. But her own hand had already beaten him to it and he ended up resting his fingers over hers. "Are you okay?" he asked.

She nodded then took a step back, her eyes darting around the lot as though she was making sure there weren't any witnesses to their interaction.

"Nobody's outside," he said as he followed her around to the driver's side of the vehicle.

Rebekah cleared her throat, but her gaze was firmly fixed on the glass double doors when she asked, "What are you doing here?"

Grant tilted his head. "You're seeing the doctor today, remember?"

"Of course I remember my appointment. I just didn't really expect you to show up."

The implication stung, but Grant forced himself to shrug it off. "I would've met you there, but I wasn't sure if your doctor's office is here in town or if you have a practitioner in Raleigh."

Back when he was a kid, visiting his aunts along with his family, there'd only been a few established doctors in Spring Forest. They hadn't needed medical services much during their trips, but he recalled one summer when his aunt Birdie had driven him to a small clinic in the older part of town for rabies shots after he'd gotten too close to a protective mother raccoon who didn't appreciate a nine-year-old Grant wanting to hold one of her babies. He knew there was now a new medical practice located in a building off Spring Forest Boulevard, but he doubted that Rebekah would use a local obstetrician and risk running into someone from town.

The muscles in her neck moved as she gulped. "Like

I said last week, you don't need to go to the actual appointment with me. I can meet you at Whole Bean Coffee afterward and fill you in."

She must've thought Grant was an idiot if she believed he would fall for that. Rebekah didn't even want to be seen in the parking lot of Furever Paws with him. No way was she going to share a coffee in public with him where anyone they knew could walk by and overhear them discussing her pregnancy. If she was going to try and outplay him, then he'd just double down on his challenge.

"Lunch sounds great. We can grab a bite to eat after we go to your appointment. Together." He held up his keys. "Should we take your car or mine?"

She did that sexy thing where she lowered her chin and tugged a corner of her lip between her teeth. Her hand gripped the driver's door handle, looking as if she was ready to yank it open and jump inside to speed away. "Why don't you just follow me?"

"And risk having you ditch me at one of the intersections?" He gave her a wink before shaking his head. "No way."

"Fine." She sighed then clicked a button on her keyless remote, electronically shutting the rear hatch of her car. "But get in quick and duck down so nobody can see you."

Grant tried not to smirk as he jogged around the front of the car to the passenger side. It was impossible for his six-foot-two frame to sink very low without jamming his knees into the glove box. Not that he would've actually hidden anyway. He understood that she didn't want anyone knowing her personal business, but he'd be damned if he was going to continue playing the role of her dirty little secret. He said as much when she tore out of the parking lot, shooting up gravel as she fishtailed onto Little Creek Road.

Rebekah made a slight chuckling sound. "That'd be a first."

"What would be?" Grant asked, finally getting his seat belt locked in.

"*You* being *my* dirty little secret," Rebekah said, the engine revving as she gained speed. "I would've thought it would be the other way around."

Something tingled along the edges of Grant's nostrils and he tried not to sniff. "Why would you be the secret?"

"Oh, come on, Grant. You're the golden boy of the Whitaker family. I just work here."

Well, the fact that she worked for his aunts wasn't the real problem bothering her right now. No, Grant heard what she wasn't saying aloud—that he might not feel comfortable going public with their...fling? Relationship? He wasn't really sure what to call their situation, but that wasn't the issue. His only concern was her feelings and assuring her that he heard her. It didn't matter how beautiful, intelligent or accomplished Rebekah was. There were always going to be some people who thought they shouldn't be together because they were different. While he couldn't deny that Rebekah's feelings were likely the result of her own experiences, he also wanted her to know that he'd always been proud to be with her. "For the record, I have never thought of you as the hired help. In fact, I'm not the one who's embarrassed to have people finding out about us."

"It's not that I'm embarrassed about you." Rebekah flicked her eyes at him before turning on her signal and pulling onto Spring Forest Boulevard. "It's that I've worked really hard to become the director of an organization that does amazing things in the community. As a nonprofit, we're governed by a different set of rules than regular corporations. That makes my job fall under more scrutiny when it comes to ensuring that everything stays aboveboard."

"So you're saying dating me wouldn't be aboveboard?"

"First of all, we're not dating." Rebekah turned to him as her car idled at an intersection. Grant tried to ignore the pang of disappointment at her words, despite the fact that he'd been telling himself exactly the same thing these past several weeks, ever since their night together. "Second of all, as you know, there's currently an attorney looking into some of your family's past investments and I don't want to risk any appearance of impropriety or otherwise suggest that there might be any conflicts of interest."

Ouch. He especially didn't like the reminder that there were potentially some financial issues going on right now with his uncle Gator.

The man had always been a financial whiz. That was why Birdie and Bunny had trusted him to manage the investments used to support their living expenses and the shelter's overhead. Gator always seemed to know just how to deal with every shift in the market, using his intelligence and intuition to help his sisters and also to build his own personal fortune. But then something had gone wrong. Suddenly money wasn't where it was supposed to be. When the storm hit Spring Forest and the shelter took heavy damage, the aunts discovered that Gator had let their insurance lapse and couldn't provide a good explanation for where the money for the premiums had gone.

The situation had seemed to get more tangled by the day, until the aunts had had no choice but to hire people to look into it. Now, Gator was nowhere to be found and some people in town were suggesting that Grant's favorite uncle had gone missing to avoid being questioned about his alleged mismanagement.

"Okay, obviously we're not dating," he readily agreed, trying to ignore the fact that there was a sour, mildew-type odor in this car that easily overpowered the scent of Rebekah's flowery lotion. "I think we both made it pretty clear that night that we weren't in the market for a serious relationship."

He certainly wasn't—especially with someone who lived a two-hour flight away. The light turned green and Rebekah barely got out a nod before pulling forward, allowing Grant to continue.

"However, with circumstances being what they are…" he glanced down to her still-flat stomach behind the seat belt "…don't you think people are going to eventually find out that you're pregnant?"

She held up a finger. "*If* I am, in fact, pregnant. Remember, the doctor hasn't officially confirmed it."

"Is there any reason to think you're not?"

The muscles in Rebekah's toned arms stiffened as

she gripped the wheel tighter. She opened her mouth as though to say something, then made a sniffing sound. "I'm not the only one who smells that, right?"

The stench that had been slowly building inside the car was becoming unbearable, and Grant finally gave in and cracked a window. "Yes, I've been smelling it for the past five minutes but was hoping it was coming from outside."

She hit a switch and both of their windows whirred all the way down. Grant inhaled the fresh, warm air filtering in as Rebekah's corkscrew curls whipped around her face. While lowering the windows improved things slightly, the scent still lingered.

"It's definitely coming from inside the car," Rebekah said, pinching her nose as she slowed for a four-way stop. "What could it be?"

"It reminds me of the time one of Aunt Birdie's goats got into the henhouse and stomped on all the eggs before rolling around in chicken poop."

"But twenty times worse," Rebekah said right before making a gagging sound.

Just then a loud yip came from somewhere in the back of the car. Grant and Rebekah nearly butted foreheads as they whipped their necks around. A mangy animal with long gray fur covering its eyes poked its head up from the storage area in the very rear of the car. The thing growled low and deep, revealing tiny yellowed teeth, and its front legs were perched on the back seat as if it was about to leap over and attack. Grant held himself perfectly still and lowered his voice. "What in the hell kind of animal is that?"

"I think it's that stray dog that everyone has been

trying to catch. Remember the one from last week that your aunt chased into the street? I've never seen it this close up, though, so I can't be sure."

"What's it doing in your car?" Grant asked.

"How should I know? It must've jumped in when I left the back hatch open to argue with you in the parking lot."

"Okay, where is your extra leash?"

Rebekah was also holding herself very still, which made her raised eyebrow even more prominent. "My extra what?"

"My aunts always keep an extra leash and a few lengths of rope in their pickup truck for this exact reason. They say they never know when they're going to come across an animal that needs help."

"Grant, just because I work at a pet rescue doesn't mean I go driving around town looking for actual pets to rescue."

The dog growled again and made a snapping motion, as if it was about to lunge at them. "Well, we probably shouldn't stay in here with him. Or her. Let's get out slowly and then I'll call an animal control officer to come take him."

Rebekah nodded. "On the count of three, we'll both get out at the same time."

Grant began the count. "One, two—" He didn't make it to three because Rebekah was already out her door.

"Oh, hell," Grant said, following suit.

Unfortunately, neither one of them realized that they'd left the windows down until the scruffy mutt launched himself over the back seat and leaped through the driver's-side window. It made a strangled yelp as it landed awkwardly on its left hind leg before it began limping across the street.

"Oh, no," Rebekah took off after the dog, calling out over her shoulder. "The poor thing is hurt."

The animal must've been more afraid than injured because when it realized Rebekah was following, it hobbled even faster, past an iron gate that had been propped open and into the yard of one of the older stately homes on Second Street.

Well, the home might've been stately at one time. It currently needed quite a bit of work involving a weed whacker, a few gallons of fresh paint and, Grant noted as he got closer, a new roof. Just as Rebekah was closing in on the scruffy pup, it found a hole in the base of the rotting porch and scurried underneath.

Grant dropped to his knees in the dried-out hydrangea bush near the hole, but it was too dark to see how far back the crawl space went. He brushed the dirt off his hands as he looked up to Rebekah. "Do you have anything we can use to bribe him out?"

Her eyes opened wider and she jogged back to the car without so much of a hint as to what she had planned.

Grant swallowed his groan. The woman certainly had a habit of doing whatever she wanted and then filling him in on the details later.

Chapter Four

Rebekah stared at the shredded bakery bag in the rear of her car. Now she knew what had lured the stray dog into becoming a stowaway. She carried the empty muffin wrapper back to the porch where Grant remained on his knees, keeping watch.

"I used to have an apple spice muffin in my tote bag, but I guess the dog already found it and had himself a picnic in the back of my car."

"Well, I'm more of a chocolate croissant kinda guy, but I can't blame the mutt for getting his baked good fixes wherever he can find them."

Something wobbled inside of Rebekah's knees. Sure, plenty of people liked chocolate croissants, but as far as she could tell, it was the first thing she and Grant had in common. In fact, she'd already had three croissants in the past week, but the bakery had been out of them this morning when she'd gone in to place her order. "I guess it's a good thing that it wasn't anything chocolate. I hear that it can make dogs really sick."

"You *hear*?" Grant lifted a brow at her.

"I've never actually owned a dog," Rebekah admitted, causing Grant to rock back onto his haunches so that he could stare at her in disbelief. "Don't look at me like that. My dad is severely allergic to them. And to cats. I wasn't able to have either growing up."

"But you work at an animal shelter."

"It's not that I don't like them or anything," Rebekah defended herself, placing her hands on her hips. "I'm just not much of a pet person."

Grant's lips lifted into a smirk. "I'm guessing this is another thing that you don't want my aunts to know about."

"Well, I'm not walking around advertising that particular fact," she said, trying to ignore his calculating gaze. Why did he always watch her as though he suspected she was hiding something? "Besides, your aunts didn't hire me to be hands-on with the animals so my experience with them isn't exactly a job requirement."

There was another growl from underneath the porch and Rebekah suddenly remembered why they were there in the first place. She held up the empty wrapper. "There's a few crumbs still stuck on here, but he pretty much licked the thing clean."

Grant stood up. "Maybe we should knock on the door and ask the owner for a treat of some kind."

Rebekah glanced at the brick house that she drove by every time she came into downtown Spring Forest. There was a smashed window on the second floor and the front screen door hung crookedly on only one hinge. "I'm pretty sure the owner no longer lives here."

"That's a shame. But it explains how the place has gotten so run-down." Grant ran a hand through his blond hair. "I've driven by a few times and always thought that it was an eyesore on this block."

Rebekah gasped. "It's not an eyesore. I mean, it could use a little bit of love and some elbow grease, but it has a ton of character. See the matching turrets that round off the front corners? None of the other mansions on this street have them. And the lot size is huge. Imagine if it had a new porch that extended all the way to here." She took several steps back and spread her arms so he could better see her vision. "Then, if I tore that rotted iron fence down, I could add a few comfy benches and make a whole seating section out here and be able to talk to my neighbors and watch kids ride their bikes and..."

Her face heated as she trailed off, mortified that she was practically admitting she'd dreamed about this particular home more than a few times—before she'd made the more practical decision to buy a smaller, more affordable townhome.

"No, don't stop," Grant said, walking closer to her. His encouraging smile and broad shoulders beneath his faded T-shirt made Rebekah grow even warmer. "Would you keep the shutters and the door the same color?"

She gulped. "I'd go with black for the shutters, but the front door I would paint a bold blue. Not quite royal blue, but not powder blue, either. Somewhere in between."

As he studied her, she realized she was describing

the exact shade of his eyes. She shivered and tried to cover it with a shrug. "But none of that matters because it's not like I'll ever own this house."

"Why not?" Grant asked. There was genuine puzzlement etched into the lines on his brow and Rebekah wondered if the guy was ever told no. Ever told that he couldn't have something he wanted.

"For one…" She held up a forefinger and tried not to notice that she was overdue for a manicure. She'd read in an online pregnancy forum that the folic acid in prenatal vitamins caused the hair and nails to grow like crazy. "Even with the house in this condition, I probably can't afford it on my salary. Second of all, if I'm having a baby, all of my money will be going for diapers and daycare and whatever else babies need. I won't have anything left over for home improvement projects."

His arms crossed in front of his chest and his entire face shifted into a frown. "You realize I'm going to help support both you and the baby, right? That means not only emotionally but financially, too."

Grant was at least wearing a pair of sneakers today instead of his normal flip-flops. But she didn't want to point out the fact that, judging by his wardrobe, she probably made more money than he did. A ring sounded from his back pocket, yet he ignored the beat-up cell phone and remained rooted in place as if he was waiting for her to respond to what he'd said.

But Rebekah didn't know what to say besides, "We should probably get to the doctor's office."

Really, there was no point in discussing any of this before they knew if she actually was pregnant. And even if she was… Grant sounded like he seriously wanted to be a part of the child's life, but Rebekah had a hard time believing it.

If a man who had been with her for six years didn't want to raise a child with her, then how could this man—who had only known her a few months—want to?

While Grant wasn't anything like her ex-boyfriend, Rebekah was also no longer like her young and naive self. She wasn't about to wait around for him to get scared and leave first—especially when her body couldn't be trusted to not react every time he smiled at her.

"Okay." He nodded, dropping his arms to his sides. "But just so you know, we will be having a conversation afterward. And maybe we can pick up another muffin or a double cheeseburger or something on our way back to lure the dog out from his hiding spot."

Rebekah's rib cage felt as if it were squeezing in on her. She cursed herself for going into work this morning to finish that grant proposal and for not taking an early lunch break. If only she'd slipped out of the office a few minutes before Grant had arrived, she could be doing this on her own, without his heavy stares and his weighty statements about taking care of her and the baby.

Grant's phone rang again when they got back into her car but he must've let the call go to voice mail because he didn't so much as glance at the thing while Rebekah drove the next couple of blocks to Dr. Singh's office.

She pretended not to be paying attention, but clearly he was making a point of proving that he was completely focused on her and not on whoever was on the other end of that phone call. Unfortunately, the short ride would've been much more bearable if he'd been distracted.

Dr. Singh's office was housed in another brick mansion on Second Avenue and the waiting room was decorated to resemble an old-fashioned parlor from the Victorian era. When Rebekah handed her insurance card over to the male receptionist, he smiled at Grant and asked, "This is Daddy, I presume?"

Rebekah's neck snapped to the velvet upholstered chaises and sofas in the small waiting room to see if the only other patient present had overheard. But the woman was struggling to keep a piece of fabric draped over her shoulder and finally threw the thing in the stroller beside her. When she met Rebekah's gaze, the lady said, "Sorry for the show, but these nursing covers are a lot more trouble than they're worth."

"No problem." Rebekah tried to smile at the breast-feeding mom, but all she could focus on were the dark circles under the woman's eyes. Rebekah's mother's eyes had often appeared equally tired after being up all night with one of the many newborns her parents had fostered over the years. Being around one crying baby after the next had easily convinced a teenaged Rebekah that motherhood wasn't for her.

So then, how had she wound up here? And with Grant, of all people? At least he'd found a seat in the corner and was politely avoiding looking at anything besides the parenting magazine he must've picked up from one of the side tables.

Thankfully, she'd saved time by completing all the

new patient forms online. How awkward would that have been to fill out her medical history chart with Grant hovering nearby?

Taking several deep breaths, she slowly trudged to where he sat and had no more than settled into a plush, emerald-green velvet chair when a woman wearing floral printed scrubs called from a doorway, "Rebekah Taylor?"

Rebekah grimaced at the use of her full name, and thereby the loss of her anonymity, then forced another fake smile as she stood up and walked toward the door.

The nurse pointed out the bathroom, then held up a small plastic cup with a lid and said, "While you give us a sample, I'll take Daddy here to the exam room."

Rebekah's head pivoted and she gasped at seeing Grant now standing behind her. When she'd told him he could come to the doctor's, she'd meant to the parking lot. Maybe as far as the lobby. Nobody had ever mentioned anything about him actually being inside the exam room with her. He must've seen the daggers her eyes were shooting because he took a step back.

"Or would you rather I wait out here?" Grant asked, and Rebekah wanted to retort that she'd prefer he waited in Jacksonville, Florida. Instead, her mouth opened and closed several times because she wasn't quite sure how to say this in front of the nurse without revealing that she'd been comfortable enough to have the man in her bed, but was not quite comfortable having him present in any other aspect of her life. When she didn't reply, Grant faced the nurse. "Is it normal for fathers to go in the exam room?"

"Very normal." The nurse nodded a bit too eagerly. "We like the daddies to be involved whenever possible. In fact, we have one patient whose husband is on deployment right now and she brings in her laptop and a webcam so he can watch via video chat. It's really the sweetest thing."

Oh, great. Rebekah should've spoken up when she had the chance. It was bad enough that the nurse was encouraging Grant to come back there with her. Now he'd think that she should broadcast all of her future appointments when he couldn't be there in person. At least he still had the courtesy to lift a questioning brow at her before barging through the door behind her.

"Fine," she sighed, then lowered her voice as they walked along the hall. "But don't you dare look when I get on the scale."

Rebekah stepped into the restroom to give her urine sample and then made her way into the exam room where Grant was staring wide-eyed at a colorful poster showing each stage of the cervix during the dilation process. She would've laughed at how pale his face had gone if the nurse hadn't pointed to a hospital-style gown and instructed Rebecca to change out of her clothes.

Grant gave a discreet cough before telling nobody in particular, "I'm just going to step down the hall and grab a drink from the water cooler."

When she was finally left alone to change, she hurriedly unzipped her dress and attempted to toss it over a nearby chair, but the thing—along with what was left of Rebekah's pride—slithered to the floor. Actually, Grant would probably need to sit in that chair anyway, since the doctor would likely use the stool. So she hung her dress on the hook behind the door, then quickly peeled off her bra and panties and wadded them into a ball to hide in her purse. She was still tying the gown closed when there was a knock on the door.

"Hi, I'm Dr. Singh," a very young woman said as she breezed into the room. "I already met Daddy outside in the hallway and he told me you guys think you're nearly nine weeks along."

Grant followed the doctor inside and Rebekah wanted to scream that there was no "you guys." There was only her. And why in the hell did everyone who worked here keep calling Grant "Daddy?" The back of her neck prickled every time she heard the presumptuous word.

But at least he'd gotten the timeline accurate.

She gulped before answering. "That's correct."

"Okay, let me pull your record up here and take a look before we get down to business." Dr. Singh logged on to a computer that was mounted on a retractable arm attached to the wall. Rebekah was relieved to note that, despite the Victorian-era waiting room, there were other modern technological advancements—such as an ultrasound machine—back here. "So on the medical history form you completed online, it says you experienced a loss of pregnancy five years ago. Tell me about that."

Rebekah's whole body went numb, as though she was frozen in a state of shock. Her eyes focused straight ahead, yet saw nothing, while her ears picked up every single sound. Including Grant's sudden indrawn breath. The wheels on the doctor's stool squeaked as Dr. Singh rolled toward her. "Rebekah? Are you not comfortable talking about this?"

She drew in a ragged gulp of air and tried not to glance at Grant to see his reaction to what she was about to admit. The paper covering the exam table shifted and crackled underneath her as she attempted to sit up straighter. "I…uh…had an ectopic pregnancy five years ago. The dose of methotrexate they gave me didn't help…dissolve, uh, anything. So they had to go in laparoscopically to remove the egg from my fallopian tube."

"I'm sorry that you went through that." Dr. Singh laid a small hand over hers and Rebekah stared at it as the initial numbness was pushed away by all the emotions now filling her. The procedure had been significantly less painful physically than it had been emotionally. At the time it happened, she'd told herself that losing the baby was for the best. That she hadn't been ready to be a mother and didn't know if she ever would be. It wasn't until right this second, surrounded by the memories of that past pregnancy, when she realized that she'd never really allowed herself to mourn that loss.

Using the sleeve of her borrowed cotton gown, she dabbed at the corner of her eye before a tear could spill out. When she finally braved a peek in Grant's direction, she saw that he was studying the pictures of the dilating cervixes with great interest.

"Well." The doctor rose to her feet. "After your past experience, I'm sure you're eager for me to check you out and give you some good news."

Dr. Singh asked routine questions as she performed a pelvic exam and took measurements of Rebekah's stomach. Grant would occasionally glance over, but mostly he stared at the wall or at the floor as he shifted in his chair and alternated which knee to bounce rapidly. It looked like the guy was seriously regretting his decision to come with her. And it served him right. Had there ever been a less interested father in this situation?

The doctor pulled a heartbeat monitor out of her pocket and squirted a blob of cold gel onto Rebekah's stomach. With the handheld machine running over her exposed skin, back and forth, Rebekah squeezed her knees together and her eyes shut, praying that if Grant *did* decide to finally show some interest, he'd keep his gaze averted to the upper half of her torso.

Not that he hadn't seen her without panties before. But this time, it was different. Not only were they currently in a clinical setting with very unflattering lights overhead, there was also a lack of lime-flavored rum to lower her inhibitions.

The machine whizzed and whirred and the doctor made some murmurs. At one point, a crease formed between the woman's dark eyebrows. "Hmm. I'm going to use the ultrasound for a better read."

Rebekah reminded herself to breathe in through her nose, out through her mouth, as more cold gel was applied to her belly. The doctor was gentle as she pushed and rotated the probe against Rebekah's stomach, which was now feeling queasy and doubly nervous.

Grant must've sensed something was wrong, as well, because he had stood up and was silently studying the screen on the ultrasound machine as though he had the training to understand what all those white squiggly lines were against the black background.

The doctor finally cleared her throat. "Excuse me for a second while I call the nurse."

* * *

Grant had seen the panic written all over Rebekah's face as the doctor took forever to perform the ultrasound. When Dr. Singh stood up to push an intercom button on the wall, he immediately reached for Rebekah's hand. She squeezed it tightly, but kept her eyes closed as she continued to take long, steady breaths.

Spending summers on his aunts' farm was the closest Grant had ever come to witnessing a birthing experience. He'd thought of picking up a book at the airport bookstore, then told himself to wait until they had more answers. But nothing he'd learned so far had prepared him for hearing about Rebekah's previous pregnancy. While she'd talked about it, her words were matter-of-fact, but her voice was shaky and he'd glanced away as soon as he saw that first tear well up. He didn't know if he should offer comfort or if he should pretend he didn't understand English. It suddenly occurred to him that the reason she'd been reluctant to discuss the pregnancy in the first place was because she wasn't sure whether or not this one would have the same result.

He stroked a thumb over her knuckle and when her eyes cracked open, he leaned closer to her ear and whispered, "I'm here for you no matter what."

The doctor resumed her place near the ultrasound machine and just when he was about to demand some answers, Dr. Singh smiled and announced, "Congratulations. You're having twins. Both of the—"

Grant didn't hear anything else except a loud bang before he crumpled to the ground.

Chapter Five

When Grant came to, Dr. Singh was kneeling beside him and the nurse was checking his pulse. Rebekah was still lying on the exam table, but was now leaning over the side and frowning at him. "So much for being here for me no matter what."

He blinked a couple more times before sitting up and rubbing at the bump forming on the back of his skull. "Did I hit my head?"

"You stepped back so quickly, you knocked into the lamp." The nurse extended her hand to help him up. "Don't worry. You're not the first dad that's happened to. Come on, big guy."

"That's why I called for the nurse." Dr. Singh took his other hand as the two medical professionals helped him to his feet. "Once I had a father faint when I told him they were having triplets."

"Did you ever have a mother pass out?" Rebekah waved her hand to get their attention. "Because it's just as startling for the half-dressed person up here on the table with cold, gooey gel everywhere."

"Sorry about that." Dr. Singh smiled as she returned to her actual patient. "So there are two strong heartbeats, both on my monitor and on the ultrasound machine."

"And they're both where they're supposed to be?" Rebekah asked hesitantly, and Grant made a mental note to research ectopic pregnancy when they left. Right after he researched twins.

Wow.

Dr. Singh nodded. "Yes. Your uterus looks great and is measuring a little bigger than what it would be for nine weeks gestation if this was a single embryo, so you're right on target for twins. Still, I'd like to do some blood work to get an idea of your hormone levels and make sure everything else checks out as normal."

Grant's head throbbed as he tried to keep up with the conversation. "So...you're sure there are *two* of them?"

"Positive. We'll be able to run more tests later in your pregnancy to determine if they're fraternal or identical. In about five or six weeks, we may even be able to determine the sex of the babies, if you're interested in finding out ahead of time."

Rebekah's eyes immediately shot to him and they were filled with shock and possibly even fear. Suddenly they'd gone from having nothing to talk about when it came to this pregnancy to having everything to talk about. Grant gently laid his hand on her shoulder, wanting to ease as much of her stress as he could. "It'll be okay," he whispered to her before turning to Dr. Singh. "I think we're going to need time to let everything sink in."

"Of course. I'm sure both of you are feeling overwhelmed right about now and nobody has to make any decisions today. But I'm going to have the nurse put together some reading material for you, and I'd like to schedule a follow-up appointment four weeks from now."

Both the doctor and nurse left the room and he and Rebekah sat there with the heavy weight of silence settling between them. Eventually it became apparent that the woman carrying his child—he shook his head, make that *children*—wasn't in any hurry to climb down from the exam table.

Finally he let the air rush out of his lungs in a deep exhaling breath that sounded like a deflating balloon. "So, twins, huh? I bet neither one of us were expecting *that*."

Rebekah shrugged, causing one side of the hospital gown to slip down and expose the very sexy curve of her shoulder. "I wasn't expecting *any* of this."

"What do you want to do?" he asked, his chest filling with an uncomfortable tension as he awaited her response.

She looked at the clock on the wall. "I guess I should go back to work."

He'd meant what did she want to do about the babies.

But she was probably still too shell-shocked to come to any sort of decision right this second.

"Well, I meant what I said about being here for you. Tell me what you need."

"I don't know what I need just yet."

"Fair enough. We'll take it one step at a time." He passed her the dress hanging on the back of the door. "Why don't you get back into your clothes and I'll wait outside."

When she met him in the hallway, she let him lead her to the front desk and even allowed him to schedule the next appointment with Dr. Singh. He asked for her car keys and she passed them to him without protest.

"Should I drive you back to your place?"

She shook her head. "No. I think I'll feel better once I get to the office and throw myself into work. Besides, you need to pick up your car."

Grant had grown up surrounded by strong women and his gut told him that Rebekah was only holding herself together because she didn't want him to witness her inability to stay in control. If he tried to push her right now, she would only close herself up more.

"Okay, I'll drive you back to the office, but only on the condition that we stop somewhere along the way and get you something to eat."

She didn't agree so much as she just didn't protest. In fact, she didn't say a word after they got into the car and he had a feeling that if she couldn't manage a conversation in the private confines of her vehicle, there was no way she'd want to step foot in a public restaurant with him. So he went to a drive-through burger place, and when he asked her what she wanted, she stared out the opposite window instead of looking at the menu board. "Whatever is fine."

He ordered for them, but she only managed a couple of French fries and a sip of sweet tea as he drove her back to work.

"Are you sure you don't want me to come inside?" he asked when he pulled into the lot at Furever Paws.

"I'm sure." Rebekah was normally so capable, so in control. Seeing her like this made Grant nervous, made him want to take a step back. Having worked as a beach lifeguard during college, Grant was accustomed to diving in headfirst at the first sign of danger.

So when he climbed into his rental car, defeat settled around him because, for the first time in his life, it felt as if he were running away from a challenge.

But how did he help someone who didn't want to be helped?

Twins.

The word replayed on a constant loop in Rebekah's head for the next hour. Despite what she'd told Grant about returning to work to clear her head, she'd been staring at the same rabies vaccine invoice since she'd gotten back to her desk.

There was no way she'd get a single bit of work done this afternoon with her mind and her nerves in such disarray. So far, she'd been able to avoid Bunny and Birdie, but she doubted that she could finish out her work day without running into Grant's aunts at least once.

A chorus of barking came from outside her office

window and she looked out to see Mollie McFadden, one of their trainers, working with two of their newest arrivals. Salt and Pepper were a bonded pair of Maltipoos that had been surrendered after their owner lost her job and couldn't afford to take them when she left to move in with her sister, who lived across the country. Seeing them suddenly reminded Rebekah of the scruffy gray dog that had jumped out of her car earlier that morning.

Standing up, she grabbed her tote bag, along with the grease-stained paper sack that still contained the now-cold burger Grant had insisted on buying for her.

"I have to go see about an animal," she told Nancy Frye, the foster coordinator who was covering at the reception desk.

Nancy was kind enough not to point out that Rebekah rarely interacted with the animals herself. Or maybe Rebekah had just raced by so quickly, Nancy hadn't gotten the chance to say anything.

In the parking lot, Richard Jackson, the veterinarian who volunteered at the shelter, lifted his arm in greeting. She managed a quick wave to the older man known as Doc J, but she didn't have the brainpower to wonder why he was stopping by when the vet clinic was already closed for the afternoon.

Rebekah started her car, the air-conditioning vents immediately blasting out the lingering scent of stale French fries and unbathed dog, and drove straight toward that old brick house on Second Avenue. She was already unwrapping the burger as she walked up to the weathered front porch.

"Here, boy," she said, awkwardly kneeling down in

her dress and heels, the cold beef patty pinched between her thumb and finger as she held it out. "Or girl. Not that it matters what I call you. You're probably just happy to have some food."

But the gray dog didn't so much as growl.

"You know, every single person at Furever Paws and probably half of the residents in this city have seen you running around on the streets. Do you know how many people have been trying to snatch you up and find you a good home? Are you still under there or did you go out on the town to scavenge your own lunch?"

Still no response.

Rebekah craned her neck toward the street to make sure some passerby wasn't watching her as she attempted to negotiate with some stray animal who probably couldn't understand a single word she was saying—and who might not even be there at all.

"Look, I didn't forget about coming back to feed you. It just took me a little longer to get here because I was in a complete daze." Rebekah groaned impatiently. "I mean, if you had any idea what kind of shock I've just been through, you'd understand why I'm standing outside some abandoned house during the hottest part of the day blabbering on and on to a stinky dog that probably isn't even under there anyway."

The muscles in her thighs began to protest her kneeling position, so she shifted until she could sit down on one of the porch steps. As much as she wanted to lure the dog out of hiding, she also didn't want it to attack her. But there was no way to get the animal to trust her unless she let down her guard slightly.

"I'm just gonna keep this yummy, all-beef patty right here next to me in case you wanna come out and have a little taste." She wrinkled her nose at the plain, cold meat that didn't look so appetizing to her without its bun or condiments. "I probably should've ordered the bacon cheeseburger. I bet you would've preferred that. But Grant was doing the ordering and I just sat there like a big dummy, too stunned to say a damn thing. I know, I know. You're probably thinking that Grant was in just as much shock as I was about the twins. But at least *he* had his escape plan already in place, conveniently having to fly back to Jacksonville this afternoon for some important meeting tonight. I mean, I guess I should be glad the man is gainfully employed. After all, everything is going to cost twice as much now that we're having twins."

The breeze picked up and she caught the now-familiar odor of stinky, wet dog, which meant the little pup must be close by. From what she'd heard, nobody had been able to get this close to the stray. Maybe if she kept talking, he or she would realize that Rebekah wasn't much of a threat.

"So, yeah. Grant took off. Just like he did the morning after we slept together. I'm not saying that he doesn't have other responsibilities. It just seems like more than a coincidence that anytime things get too heavy, he always has an easy out and can pick up and leave whenever he wants. You should've seen him today in the doctor's office. The second she told us it was twins, he stepped back from me so fast that he hit his head on a lamp and all but collapsed. It actually would've been hilarious if I wasn't so damn scared myself, let me tell you.

"I don't care how hot the guy is. Or how my insides turn all gooey every time I see him. This attraction will wear off eventually." Rebekah dug around inside the carry-out bag for a cold French fry. All this talking was finally bringing back her appetite. "But it certainly doesn't bode well for our children if their father can't even handle the first surprise of the pregnancy. Not that I handled it all that well myself." She bit into the top half of the soggy fry. "Bleh."

She tossed the remainder to the dirt near the hole under the porch where she'd seen the dog scurry earlier today. She could've sworn she heard something rustling around down there, but it could've just as easily been a squirrel. Or a rat. Or a snake. Before Rebekah could think about what other critters might've burrowed their way under there, she heard the Bluetooth ringing from her car.

She had no idea how long she'd been sitting here, but her mom had been calling her every day this week after school let out to make sure everything was ready for her class's field trip to the animal rescue next Tuesday. At this point, it was almost like a regularly scheduled alarm, letting her know that it was close to four o'clock.

Rebekah stood up and brushed the dirt off her rear end. She set the burger down near her discarded French fry and grabbed her trash. "You win," she told the little gray dog, or whichever other animal was under the porch. "I've gotta go call my mom back and tell her the news. Wish me luck."

There wasn't even a yip in thanks as she made her way across the potholed driveway and toward her car. But as Rebekah pulled away from the curb, she caught a glimpse of gray fur darting out of the hole and then back under the porch.

Apparently, the scruffy little mutt had been listening to her the whole time.

The following week, as the flight attendant made her safety presentation over the loudspeaker of the plane, Grant paid very close attention despite the fact that he could probably give the exact speech by heart. He'd flown so much recently, and the constant traveling was beginning to take its toll on him. Or maybe it was the added stress of knowing that he was going to be a father that had him feeling so shaky.

As the plane accelerated down the runway, he performed the same ritual he always did at the beginning of a flight. He closed his eyes, rotated his neck, pushed back his shoulders, adjusted his arms, stretched out his fingers. Deep breath. Then he extended his legs as far as they would go in the business class row and rolled his ankles in counter-clockwise circles before finishing with the wiggling of his toes. Another deep breath.

Repeat.

It wasn't that he was superstitious, but the familiar routine helped him to relax. He'd been a nervous flyer ever since he was eight years old. That had been the first summer he'd flown all by himself to visit his dad's sisters in North Carolina and his plane had hit major turbulence. Then there was the summer he was ten and an unexpected hurricane diverted his flight and he'd been stuck at the airport in Nashville with only a handful of airline employees. He hadn't confided his fears to anyone, mostly because he'd had such an amazing time on his aunts' farm those years and knew that if anyone thought he couldn't brave another flight as an unaccompanied minor, he might not get to visit again. Then his younger sisters began accompanying him and he'd been forced to become the brave knowledgeable brother.

But he still didn't like planes.

So while he loved his marketing job and his amazing company, there were definitely days when he wished he could travel a lot less. When they finally reached cruising altitude, he powered on his tablet and read his downloaded copy of *What to Expect When You're Expecting.*

"Is that book still around?" the passenger next to him asked.

Grant had to blink a few times before he figured out what the middle-aged gentleman in the loud Hawaiian-print shirt had said.

The guy nodded toward Grant's iPad and said, "My wife made me read the same book way back when."

"Any advice you can give me?"

"Yeah. No matter how well you plan, there's always going to be something that comes up to throw you for a loop." The man chuckled before adding, "After having twenty-eight newborns, I still get a curveball thrown my way every once in a while."

"You have twenty-eight kids?" Grant hoped his eyes weren't completely bugging out of his head.

"Well, technically, we just have one. A daughter.

Smart as a whip and pretty as a peach. But my wife and I were foster parents and we used to get all the calls for the newborns. So we've had a lot of babies in and out of our house over the years."

"By any chance, were any of them twins?"

"Oh, boy. Is that what you and your wife are having?" the man asked, then glanced down at Grant's bare ring finger.

"My girlfriend," Grant clarified. Okay, so technically, Rebekah wasn't exactly his girlfriend, either. But some stranger on a plane didn't necessarily need those kinds of specifics.

Just then, a baby a few rows back began fussing and the man looked behind them. "Poor thing. Probably has plugged ears from the altitude. So, how far along is your girlfriend?"

"Almost ten weeks. Here's the ultrasound picture from our first appointment." Grant swiped his finger across his tablet to go to his stored photos. He'd taken a screenshot of the printout Dr. Singh had given them, but since Rebekah hadn't wanted to tell anyone yet, Grant hadn't said a word to his family or to anyone at work.

He didn't realize how eager he'd been to finally show the picture to someone until the older man said, "Yep. There's two of them, all right."

The baby's cries picked up volume and a whiny toddler joined in. Several passengers near them adjusted their earphones or sent the mother of the fussy children pointed looks.

"Excuse me," the man said, unsnapping his seat belt and standing up. Grant had to rise to let the man pass.

Since Grant hated the views from window seats, he always asked to be assigned to the aisle. He remained on his feet, observing Hawaiian Shirt Guy speak quietly to the young mother before gently taking the baby into his arms. The crying immediately ceased and the young mom was able to focus her attention on the toddler next to her.

Grant sat back down, then watched in awe the rest of the flight as this miracle stranger did a bouncing/rocking motion while pacing up and down the aisle until the baby rested its chubby cheek against the man's shoulder and fell soundly asleep. When it was time to begin their descent, the mom worried that transferring the finally calmed child might wake her up so Grant slid over to the window seat—after shutting the shade—allowing the man to take the aisle seat closer to the mom. Hawaiian Shirt Guy made it all seem so effortless as he gently shifted the baby to his other shoulder, then sat down and got his seat belt back on without so much as an eye flutter from the tiny girl now drooling all over the palm tree fronds printed on his shirt.

"Have you thought of writing a book of your own?" Grant asked his seatmate when the plane touched down.

The older guy just laughed. "The thought has crossed my mind a time or two."

"Or you could give private lessons," Grant suggested. "I'd pay anything to learn how to do that."

"You'll figure it out on your own, son. Just the fact that you *want* to get it right already speaks volumes about the kind of father you'll be."

As the rest of the passengers raced each other to reach the overhead compartments and line up for the exit, the tiny girl with black curls and a lopsided pink headband finally opened her eyes. Grant prepared his ears for a sudden shriek that was sure to come when the baby realized that neither the man in front of her nor the one holding her was her mother. But the baby quickly smiled at him, revealing one tiny white tooth in her otherwise gummy grin, and Grant felt his heart turn into a puddle.

Would his own children ever smile at him that way? Would their mother?

The man beside him stood up and passed the baby off to a very grateful mom, but Grant remained in place, a million thoughts running through his head. What would being a father really be like? His own dad had set the bar pretty high when it came to being an amazing parent, but Moose Whitaker had passed away right after Grant graduated high school and was no longer around to offer that sound advice he'd always happily dished out. Whether it was an intimidating wave or a midterm exam in calculus, Moose had always known the right thing to say to inspire Grant to conquer his biggest challenges.

He was so lost in thoughts about parenthood, he didn't realize the plane had emptied and the flight attendants were letting the cleaning crew aboard. He yanked his carry-on suitcase from the overhead bin and made his way to the rental car desk. The clerk on duty greeted him by name and Grant realized that his visits to North Carolina were coming with increasing frequency.

During the forty-five-minute drive to Spring Forest, he made several work-related calls and told himself that as long as he still handled his job duties, it didn't matter how much time he spent out of the office. Which was a good thing since, with all of Rebekah's upcoming doctor's appointments and birthing classes and whatever else people did to prepare for a baby, he'd be racking up even more frequent flyer miles.

Speaking of which, he should probably come up with another excuse to give his aunts for why he was in town again so soon. The truth was that he wanted to check on Rebekah, but he couldn't very well tell them that. Hell, he couldn't even tell Rebekah that.

When he turned into the parking lot at Furever Paws, his eyes immediately landed on the same Hawaiian-print shirt that he'd sat next to on the plane. Certainly, it couldn't be the same guy, he told the knot of tension forming in his belly.

But, sure enough, as Grant exited his car, he recognized the man who was now standing near an older-model Subaru Outback and tearing into a pack of Claritin. His former seatmate swallowed some pills and then grabbed a floppy hat out of his back seat before waving at Grant. "I hope you didn't follow me all the way out here to ask for more baby advice."

Grant's lips tightened as he looked around to see if anyone had heard the man's words. "No, actually, my aunts own this place."

Please don't ask about the woman I told you was my girlfriend.

"Oh, Bunny and Birdie are your aunts? My daughter thinks the world of them. In fact, I'm meeting her and my wife here for lunch." The man jerked a thumb at the big yellow school bus lumbering into the driveway. "And there's my wife now. Our daughter arranged for this field trip for my wife's first-grade class and neither one of them thought I'd make it back from my book tour in time to help chaperone. Good thing our plane landed early, huh?"

The man walked over to the bus that was idling on the edge of the property before Grant could ask him who his daughter was. But he didn't have to.

Because, just then, Rebekah came walking up from the side of the building, her wide smile indicating she hadn't yet seen Grant frozen between the two cars. The bus's engine shut off right as she began speaking.

"I didn't know you were coming." She threw her arms around the man's shoulders, nearly knocking off his floppy hat. "I hope you brought some extra-strength allergy medicine with you, Daddy."

Chapter Six

"I need to talk to you," Grant whispered to Rebekah as she passed out clipboards to the parent chaperones who were herding the schoolchildren into groups named after animals.

Thankfully, she had on her sunglasses and nobody could see her squeeze her eyes shut at the sound of his voice. His breath was so close to her ear, she nearly shuddered. "What are you doing here, Grant?"

"I wanted to get some pictures of the new picnic area so I could add it to the brochures I'm creating."

"What brochures?" Rebekah's smile fell. "I never authorized the money for any new brochures."

"We can talk about that later." His voice was still low and laced with an edge of desperation. "Right now, I really need to speak to you about...*you know.*"

"Here you go." She handed a clipboard to another parent chaperone and forced a smile, trying to pretend that the father of her babies wasn't standing directly behind her while her own parents were only a few feet away. "Your group will be called the Ducks and your tour guide is going to be Hans, the silver-haired gentleman over there wearing the purple shirt."

As the Duck group headed off, Rebekah looked anywhere but at Grant and spoke through clenched teeth. "Now is not a good time to talk about...*you know*. Not only am I working, but it just so happens that those are my parents over there."

"That's exactly why we need to talk about—"

"Here you go." She cut Grant off again as she reached out to hand another clipboard to a man who had lost all control over six girls, who were now running in circles and trying to play tag. "Your group will be called the Frogs and your tour guide is going to be—"

"I don't want to be a frog," a little girl with box braids said.

"Why can't we be called the unicorns?" another little girl with a blond ponytail right above her forehead asked. "See? I already have a unicorn horn and everything."

"I'd rather be a Tyrannosaurus rex," a third girl said, pushing a pair of blue-framed glasses up on her nose. "A T. rex could probably eat a unicorn, you know."

"Could not," the blonde retorted, putting her hands on her hips.

The remaining three girls stopped their impromptu game of tag to join in the argument of dinosaurs versus mythical creatures and Rebekah decided right then and there that she would never organize another field trip again. She tried to wave her mom over, hoping the experienced Mrs. Taylor would be able to get her students to stop their bickering. But her mother was several yards away, introducing the other two teachers to Doc J, who would be giving the classes a tour of the vet clinic.

"Technically..." Grant raised his voice, stepping directly into the center of the fray "...T. rexes are carnivores, which means they only eat meat. And unicorns are made out of rainbows and fairy glitter and wouldn't be at all tasty to a meat-loving T. rex. Fairy glitter is way too sweet. Bleh." Grant made a shuddering sound and all the girls laughed. He winked at Rebekah before continuing. "Since there were no such things as dinosaur dentists back then and a T. rex's arms were obviously too short to get a toothbrush into those hard to reach spots, eating a unicorn wouldn't have been at all worth the risk of so many cavities."

"Are you sure?" The little girl with glasses was also wearing a T-shirt displaying the periodic table on it and didn't quite looked convinced.

"Of course I'm sure." Grant nodded and pulled out his cracked smartphone. "In fact, I'm pretty sure that an archaeologist once found some cave drawings showing a dinosaur and a unicorn being friends. I'll look for pictures of them while you guys start your field trip."

"I still don't want to be a frog, though," the original little girl said, crossing her arms in front of her.

Grant grabbed the clipboard from Rebecca and took the pen that was attached to the metal clasp. He scribbled something out and then wrote something else before handing the clipboard over to the dad whose skeptical facial expression probably mirrored Rebekah's.

"Now you guys are the Uni-rexes." Grant wiggled his eyebrows at them. The girls all squealed in delight and ran off toward the volunteer tour guides stationed near the picnic tables.

"Very well done." The sudden sound of her mother's voice behind them caused Rebekah to startle. "My husband tells me that you're Bunny and Birdie's nephew."

Grant's Adam's apple bobbed up and down as he gulped, his wide eyes darting between Sheila and Mike Taylor. Was he surprised to see that her parents were polar opposites—at least in terms of appearance? Her father's graying red hair and light complexion were protected from the harsh effects of the sun by his dorky hat. Her mother's hair was black and had a natural curl—not a single gray hair to be seen—while her smooth skin was a dark umber, set off by the bright colors of her cotton tunic. It clashed horribly with the Hawaiian-print shirt her dad always wore when he was traveling to promote one of the many books he'd written about his adventures in fatherhood.

Growing up as a biracial child, Rebekah became accustomed to people doing double takes at her parents, trying to figure out which one she resembled more. She resisted the urge to put a protective hand over her belly as she wondered whether her own children would face that same experience. Perhaps Grant was wondering the exact same thing. She could see the beads of perspiration forming on his brow and, despite the fact that it was still warm in mid-September, she had a feeling his discomfort was due to this unexpected meeting.

No doubt he was wishing he could be anywhere but here. Again.

He cleared his throat as he answered Rebekah's mother. "That's correct, ma'am. I'm Grant Whitaker."

He held out his hand and her mother grasped it with both of hers. "So, do you work with Rebekah?"

He opened his mouth then closed it. Then he glanced at his rental car before turning to Rebekah and allowing his gaze to dart down toward her waist.

"Sort of," he said, causing her stomach to sink under his pointed gaze. Her lips remained in a firm line as her eyes pleaded with him not to say anything more. Where was the calm, laid-back Grant who'd scheduled her next doctor's appointment when Rebekah was in a daze, or the take-charge and creative one who invented Uni-rexes for arguing little girls? She could certainly use some of that creativity to spin a story right now.

Because her parents were now staring at both of them while she and Grant stared at each other, Rebekah had to jump in and say something. "Grant works in Jacksonville."

He immediately nodded. "That's right. I work in Jacksonville. And I live there. I live *and* work in Jacksonville. Florida."

"Then that explains why you were on my flight," her dad replied. He turned to his wife. "Grant and I sat together on the plane."

"We hadn't officially met, though." Grant rocked

back on his heels and took a deep breath. His blue eyes had gone a shade darker and his normally tan face had gone a shade paler. "So I had no idea that he was your dad, Rebekah."

What did that mean? Was he trying to apologize for something? It didn't seem like he'd been rude to her father—in fact, they seemed to be getting along well. So what was the problem? A knot formed in her chest as she looked between Grant and her dad, who was now smiling.

"When I saw him reading the *What to Expect When You're Expecting* book, I struck up a conversation and gave him some advice about fatherhood." Her dad put a hand on Grant's shoulder. When he turned to his wife, Rebekah tried not to bite all the way through her lip as he continued. "Grant's girlfriend is pregnant with twins. Isn't that exciting?"

And that was when her own forehead broke out in a cold sweat.

Grant knew by her wide eyes filled with remorse that Rebekah hadn't told her parents yet about the pregnancy.

As they stood in the parking lot of the animal shelter with the midmorning sun beating down on them and the excited voices of about fifty first graders echoing all around, Mrs. Taylor took one look at her daughter and her smile dropped. Guilt was written all over Rebekah's face—and if Grant could read it that clearly after only knowing her for a short time, it must be completely obvious to her parents. Grant couldn't help but think all of this could've been avoided if only she'd told them.

Or if he hadn't gotten antsy waiting around for her to call and hopped on that flight this morning.

"Are you…" Sheila Taylor began to ask her daughter, her dark eyes darting down to Rebekah's midsection.

Rebekah sighed and put her forehead in her palm. She didn't look at either parent when she answered, "I was going to tell you both this weekend."

"Tell us what?" Mike Taylor asked, and his wife used her elbow to nudge him in the ribs. He squinted one eye at where Sheila was staring and then his head pivoted to Grant.

"My *daughter's* your girlfriend?"

Rebekah gasped. "Well, technically, we're not—"

"It's complicated," Grant interrupted and put a protective arm over Rebekah's shoulders. "But we're working things out."

"Oh, my gosh." Sheila covered her mouth and her eyes grew damp. "So we're going to be grandparents?"

"And it's twins." Mike clapped his hands together. "That means double the fun."

"Twins!" His wife gripped his upper arm. "I'm going to need to get the bassinet back out of the garage."

"And the baby swing." Mike giggled as he lifted his wife up in a quick hug. Then he locked Rebekah into a bear hug before releasing her to pivot back to Sheila. "Or did we get rid of it a few years ago? If so, we're gonna need to get another one."

"Two," Grant said holding up two fingers. He immediately felt Rebekah's elbow against his rib cage.

Like mother, like daughter, apparently. "What? I'm just pointing out that we're going to need two of everything."

One of the parent chaperones yelled for Mrs. Taylor and she waved back. "Okay. I have to go supervise the field trip. But, oh, my gosh. We're going to have so much to do. This is so exciting." Then the woman pointed at Grant. "Don't go anywhere. We'll have dinner tonight to celebrate."

"Yes, ma'am," he told her and braced himself for another tight-lipped frown from Rebekah.

But she was being swept up in another hug by her father. "I can't believe my little Dimples is gonna be a mom. This is so exciting."

"We'll talk more about it later, Dad." Rebekah seemed as if she was trying to smile, but Grant could see the expression didn't quite reach her eyes. "You better go help Mom and that poor parent who got stuck chaperoning the Frog group."

It was actually the Uni-rex group now, but Grant didn't think Rebekah would appreciate the correction right that second. When her parents walked away, she lowered her face into her palms. Grant placed a hand on her lower back and rubbed slow circles. "Are you feeling okay? Do you need to throw up?"

"I'm too busy to throw up." Rebekah finally lifted her eyes to him. "I have to oversee a field trip for fifty kids, I have a tour group from the city council's office coming this afternoon to see our plans for where we plan to place the cell tower and I have a budget meeting with your aunts at five. Oh, and now my parents want to have dinner with us and probably quiz me about the status of our nonexistent relationship."

"Nonexistent? Ouch."

"You know what I mean, Grant. You yourself called it complicated." Rebekah used her fingers to massage the deep crease forming right above her nose. If she hadn't looked like she was about to hyperventilate, her reaction might've actually been considered cute. Oh, who was he kidding? Even overwhelmed and frustrated, Rebekah Taylor was still a mighty attractive woman. Too bad all of that frustration was currently directed at him. "This was *not* the way I wanted them to find out."

"I tried to tell you that we needed to talk," he reminded her. "Once I realized who your father was, I wanted to warn you."

"You could've just waited for me in my office," she suggested.

"Your dad had already seen me in the parking lot. Then, when they came over, I was trying to think of a fast way to throw them off the topic while simultaneously hoping your dad would have forgotten what I'd said on the plane."

"Is that what you were doing? You went all pale and looked so nervous, I thought you were going to faint again like you did in Dr. Singh's office."

"I didn't faint," he defended himself. "I knocked myself out. By accident." Okay, so even he knew that was lame.

She rolled her eyes. "Whatever. The only thing I've asked from you through all of this is to keep it under wraps until I was ready to tell people. And you couldn't even handle that."

The hurt in her tone hung between them and his heart hammered as he schooled his features and woodenly returned Mike Taylor's thumbs-up gesture from across the parking lot.

She had a point. Sure, he'd talked to a stranger—uh, sort of—on a plane, and not the editor of the *Spring Forest Gazette.* But he had made her a promise, and he could see why she felt betrayed. Now he needed to make things right. To show her that she could trust and depend on him.

"Again, I didn't know the stranger sitting next to me on the plane was your father."

Grant watched Rebekah cross her arms over her chest, which only served to thrust her attractive breasts up higher. "Besides, you said you were planning to tell them last weekend. I had no way of knowing that you hadn't gone through with it. But now they've found out, and while I obviously don't know them as well as you do, they seemed to take it well enough."

"The fact remains that I wasn't ready for the whole world to know I was pregnant just yet. And I especially wasn't ready for them to know that you're the father."

"What's wrong with me being the father?"

"Can we not do this here?" Rebekah wouldn't meet his gaze and the sting from her earlier comment about him not being able to handle his side of the bargain intensified. "There's your Aunt Birdie. I know she and Bunny will figure things out eventually, but I would like to keep my personal life and my work life separate for as long as possible. Let me deal with my parents and you keep your aunts occupied today so they don't find out from my dad, who is probably already on the phone with his publicist trying to score free samples of all the latest baby gear."

Rebekah walked away, her desire to keep their relationship a secret leaving a bad taste in his mouth. Wait, she'd specifically told him that they didn't have a relationship—secret or otherwise. And while he knew she was upset, that was still a little more than he was willing to stomach. It wasn't as if he was feeling the urge to settle down and get married, himself. But they were going to be in each other's lives for at least the next eighteen-plus years, so she'd better figure out pretty quickly how to explain his presence to people. And not blame him for every single thing that she couldn't control.

Screw it. If she didn't want anything to do with him, then he'd give her exactly what she wanted. She could keep her secret and protect her precious reputation and go at it alone.

Grant was about to walk back to his car and drive to the airport when Aunt Birdie interrupted his thoughts. "She's a wonder, isn't she?"

"She's something, all right," Grant replied, not taking his eyes off Rebekah.

"The girl has been a blessing to the shelter. Not only does she keep us organized, but she's full of all these big ideas for bringing awareness to our adoption program. This field trip was her idea and if today goes well, we're gonna partner up with some of the local schools and get more kids out here for a hands-on learning experience about animals."

"Hmm" was all he could manage in response. He wasn't really in the mood to hear every single one of Rebekah's praiseworthy attributes when was currently trying to pretend that he didn't exist.

"I heard you two went out for drinks together a couple months back." Birdie was more direct than her sister, and her eyes narrowed behind her glasses. "I've been hoping that meant you were getting along better now."

"What makes you think we don't get along, Aunt Birdie?"

His aunt answered by rolling her eyes and using a bobby pin to adjust the already tidy gray bun on top of her head. "So, what brings you to Spring Forest today, son?"

Grant couldn't very well admit that he'd flown out here purposely to see Rebekah. And after her comment about his fainting in the doctor's office and the accusation that he hadn't kept her pregnancy a secret, he decided that this was the perfect opportunity to prove to her that he could handle anything she threw his way. Besides, he had an excuse prepared—the same one he'd given Rebekah earlier. "I was actually going to take some pictures of that new picnic area for a brochure I'm working on."

Birdie's smile lit up her face and she put a wrinkled and work-roughened hand on his biceps. "A brochure would be fantastic. We could hand them out at adoption events or when we do our booth at the annual street fair. Why are you always so good to your old aunties, Grant?"

See, Rebekah wasn't the only one who could come up with innovative ideas. And it wasn't just a cover story— he really did want to do all he could for his aunts and for the shelter that meant so much to them.

It was no secret that when his Whitaker grandparents had died, they'd left all their property to their four children in equal shares. His father had sold off his first, while his Uncle Gator had held on to his and then reaped a financial windfall by selling when the market was at its peak. Birdie and Bunny were the last two to own parcels of Whitaker Acres, yet their money had been so mismanaged recently, they'd hired an attorney to look into the possibility of recouping some of their losses. In the meantime, he'd been the one to suggest the possibility of leasing land to some of his contacts in the wireless industry for a cell tower, as well as any other money-producing ventures he could think of to keep his aunts' rescue shelter afloat.

Grant slipped Birdie's hand into the crook of his arm and led her to the building's entrance. "I also wanted to pick your and Bunny's brains on the possibility of doing a big gala here as a fund-raiser."

"Like a fancy dress-up party?"

"Well, not too fancy. But we could have dinner and dancing and maybe a silent auction. And people can bring their pets in dress-up costumes. When I was at my conference in San Francisco, the hotel where I stayed was hosting something similar. They called it a Fur Ball."

"A Fur Ball!" Birdie clapped her hands. "Wait until I tell Rebekah."

"Let's not bother her right now while she has her hands full with the field trip kids. I'll take you and Aunt Bunny to the Main Street Grille and we can talk about it. If Amanda Sylvester is there, we can ask her about catering the event. Maybe we can add on to the picnic area and create an outdoor party space."

Grant had no idea where any of this was coming from, but he kept talking about any innovation he could think of as he steered the older woman toward the office. Hopefully, he could grab his other aunt and then get them far away before the field trip ended. He shuddered to think of what Rebekah's reaction would be if her parents ran into the aunts and completely blew their secret.

Rebekah didn't know where Grant had gone, but she didn't take an easy breath until her dad's old Subaru was long gone and the school bus had rumbled out of the parking lot after lunch. Her mom was only twenty minutes down the road when she sent a text asking where they should make a reservation for dinner tonight with Grant.

She shot back a quick reply saying she'd talk to Grant. Rebekah would let him be the one to come up with an excuse about why they couldn't come to Raleigh tonight for dinner.

When she finally finished her tour with the city council members later that afternoon and they'd driven off, she realized there weren't any cars left in the parking lot that she didn't recognize. That was weird, considering Grant always rented one when he came to town.

She went to her office and gobbled down one of the banana-nut muffins she'd been too busy—and nervous—to eat earlier. It was a little stale from sitting on her desk all day, but her stomach was growling in protest. She took a few quick bites as she made printouts of the budget reports she'd prepared for her bosses. However, when Bunny and Birdie arrived at her office, they barely glanced at their pages of detailed line item numbers, since they were too busy talking about all of Grant's latest ideas for something called a Fur Ball.

"And if the gala goes well, we could possibly start hosting bigger events," Birdie told her.

"Like weddings," Bunny added. "That could really bring in some much needed revenue."

"But we're a nonprofit animal shelter," Rebekah tried to remind them. "I think there might be tax ramifications if we turn the place into some sort of party venue."

"That's why we have you to look into all this for us. Grant said you'd know who to talk to about stuff like that."

Oh, had he now? Rebekah felt her unappeased hunger give way to annoyance.

"Um, speaking of your nephew," Rebekah sneaked a peek at her phone screen, which had two new text notifications from her dad. "Is he still around?"

The two sisters looked at each other quickly before turning their faces to Rebekah.

"Did you want to talk to him about something?" Bunny asked. She was the more absentminded of the

Whitaker sisters. Very sweet, but usually had her head in the clouds. There was no way the woman would have reason to think something was up.

"Um… I only wanted to talk to him about the pictures he was going to use for the brochures."

"Oh, he got some great ones of the kiddos sitting on the new wooden bleachers Bobby Doyle built. Doc J had the llamas out and half the class was raising their hands wanting to ask questions. He said he'd email the photos to us when he gets back to Jacksonville tonight."

Rebekah's head jerked back. "He went home already?"

The sisters shared another look and she realized she needed to get her emotions under lock and key. She certainly didn't want them knowing that their precious nephew was supposed to be having dinner tonight with her parents so they could all talk about the pregnancy nobody was supposed to know about yet.

"I mean, I figured he was leaving, but I wanted to make sure none of his shots showed the children's faces. We would need signed release waivers to publish their images and…uh…we'd probably rather not have to deal with that entire legal headache."

"Well, why don't you call him?" Birdie, the more sensible and pragmatic sister, asked. "His plane should've landed by now."

Her bosses stared at her expectantly and Rebekah was relieved that her answer was completely honest when she sank back in her seat and said, "I don't have his number."

Birdie rattled off the digits and then they both sat

there as though they had no intention of leaving until Rebekah actually called the man. There was no way she was going to have a conversation with Grant in front of the women. Who knew what the guy might say? Or what her own facial expressions might give away?

"Why don't I just send a text? That way, I'm not bothering him if he's still at the airport and he can respond whenever it's convenient for him."

The ladies still didn't budge, so Rebekah somehow managed to keep her fingers from trembling as she typed in the number and then wrote a quick message asking about the pictures for the brochures. She pressed Send and the whooshing sound echoed in the office.

She used her thumb to discreetly set her device to vibrate and then shoved it deep in her purse, just in case Grant responded and his aunts wanted to know what he'd said. "So, I'd better be off. I've got to drive to Raleigh tonight and have dinner with my parents."

"Oh, no." Bunny scratched at a loose gray curl near her temple. "We didn't get to talk to your mom while she was here. Grant kept us out and about all day. He even took us by that old house on Second Street where he thinks the little gray dog might be hiding."

Rebekah was already on her feet and shoving her laptop into her tote bag when her ears perked. "Did you guys see him?"

"How do you know it's a him?" Birdie asked.

"Or her." Rebekah quickly corrected. She actually had no idea what gender the thing was but she'd been leaving little treats near that same porch every day and, with the exception of the soy bacon she'd accidentally ordered last Sunday at brunch, all of the food was gone the next day. So the dog—or whatever other wild creature lived under there—definitely had a healthy appetite.

"Nope." Bunny shook her head. "No sign of the little dear."

It wasn't until Rebekah was out in her car that she realized Grant had actually followed through with something besides showing up for her doctor's appointment. He'd kept his aunts occupied all day so that her parents didn't see them and accidentally reveal anything about her pregnancy.

Maybe the guy could be useful, after all.

Chapter Seven

As soon as the plane landed and he powered on his phone, Grant saw a text from an unknown number. When he realized it was from Rebekah, he smiled as triumph coursed through his body. She might be talking about business stuff and legal releases, but at least he now had her number.

Taking whatever minor victories he could get at this point, he typed in a reply.

Don't worry. All of the pictures I took showed the kids facing away from me. I may not know much about babies, but I know all about marketing and licensing agreements.

Not expecting a response, he was surprised when he got to the long-term parking garage and felt his phone vibrate in his pocket.

Thanks for keeping your aunts busy today. You filled their heads with lots of crazy talk about Fur Balls and animal-themed weddings, but at least they don't suspect anything about us.

He wanted to tell her that she couldn't keep the babies a secret forever. Instead, he wrote,

Sorry for bailing out before dinner with your parents tonight. I figured you'd prefer me not being there to make things even more awkward, but I still hope you'll make my apologies to Mike and Sheila.

A few dots appeared, indicating she was typing something, then they disappeared. When he got to a stoplight, he saw a new text from her.

Yeah. Awkward is one word for it.

Now that he finally had her texting him, he wanted to keep the conversation going. But a horn sounded behind him and he had to drive.

When he pulled into the underground parking garage at his condo complex, he saw that she'd sent a follow-up message.

To be honest, I also bailed out on dinner. It's been a long day and I need more time to prepare myself for all their questions.

The reception down here was nonexistent (like their relationship), so Grant waited until he'd let himself into his condo to respond. He stood in front of the floor-to-ceiling sliding glass doors that looked out over the Atlantic Ocean, but he didn't notice the view because he was too busy staring at the electronic keyboard on his screen. Finally he typed, If you want, I can fly back this weekend and face them with you.

Thanks for the offer, but I think having you there would only make me more flustered.

So I fluster you. He added the winking emoji then pressed Send.

Of course. Her reply caused a burst of satisfaction to swell through his chest. His pulse sped up. Then a second bubble appeared right after. The whole situation has me all out of sorts.

Grant knew that her addendum was an understatement. He'd also been thrown for a loop when he'd found out they were having twins. While they'd both been active participants that night and had taken steps to prevent this exact thing, he only had to deal with the mental and emotional aspects of her pregnancy. Rebekah had the added physical and hormonal burden.

I was reading that stress isn't good for the babies. Is there anything I can do to make things easier?

He expected her to tell him to stay as far away from her as possible. Instead, she answered, Go to dinner with my parents on my behalf.

He was about to tell her that he'd book a flight right then, but she immediately added, I'm only kidding. I'm sure once I get through their interrogation this weekend, it'll get easier telling everyone else.

Then let me help prep you for all their questions.

What do you mean?

I'll pretend I'm your parents and ask you whatever parents would ask in a situation like this.

Grant collapsed on his leather sofa while he waited for her reply. He could almost imagine the sound of her breathless sigh as she wrote, Fine.

Okay. First question. What's your due date?

Easy. March 1. But sometimes twins come early.

They do?

Is this a question from you, Grant? Because I'm pretty sure my parents know everything there is to know about babies. Even twins. My mom has a master's in early childhood development and my dad has published several books on newborns and being a foster father.

Grant stood up to retrieve his iPad out of the backpack he'd left near his carry-on suitcase. He opened the internet search engine and typed in the name Mike Taylor. Her dad's picture popped up along with links to several of his bestselling books. No wonder the guy had laughed at Grant's suggestion on the flight.

Sorry. I've only had time to scan through some of the reading material Dr. Singh had suggested and I must've missed that part.

He started to type that he wished her dad had clued him in when they'd been on the airplane together, but it was probably best not to remind her about his accidental information leak in the first place.

All right, back to THEIR questions. Are you going to find out the genders?

I think I'm going to want to know the closer it gets to the due date. You know I'm a planner and like to be prepared for everything ahead of time.

Grant let out a whoosh of air. That was good to know. Personally, he was dying to find out if they were going to have girls or boys. Or one of each. Since they hadn't really had the chance to open up with each other and discuss it, this role-playing-via-text thing was actually working out in his favor. But it would only succeed if he legitimately sounded as though he was channeling her parents and asking questions they would ask their daughter. Which was difficult because the only thing he knew about the Taylors was that they lived in Raleigh and they were apparently experts when it came to babies.

He returned to his internet search on his iPad and typed, *biggest issues for new parents*. An article entitled "Breastfeeding versus Bottle" popped up and Grant quickly turned the device off. Nope. There was no way he was going to ask Rebekah anything about her breasts. At least, not yet. Although, he did like to think about them often. "No, focus," he told himself.

We can't wait to hold our grandbabies. If you move back home, we can help take care of them.

He pressed Send, then wondered if that sounded too over the top. But surely her parents would want to be close to their new grandchildren.

I would love for you guys to help out on the weekends, but I'm happy at my job and my home is in Spring Forest.

Her townhome was nice, but it was one of the smaller units with only two bedrooms. And if Grant remembered correctly, one of those bedrooms was set up as her office.

You'll probably need more space when the babies get older. Maybe a place with a yard.

He remembered the way she'd looked when she was talking about the old brick house on Second Avenue and he wondered if she was thinking about that exact yard. Finally, she replied,

Well, I'll have to see what I can afford when the time comes.

Speaking of money, what about the father? What's his name again? Greg?

Grant. Her response could've been keeping to their roles, or it could have been her rolling her pretty hazel eyes at him—meaning *knock it off and be serious.*
So he quickly added,

Well, we're sure this Grant guy is going to help you out financially. He seems like a responsible and dependable sort who wants to be active in his children's lives. And he's incredibly handsome.

She didn't respond for a few minutes and Grant walked over to his kitchen to grab a beer. His fridge contained three Coronas, two expired containers of yogurt his sister had dropped off when she'd delivered some groceries over a month ago and a nearly black banana from one of the boxed lunches he usually brought home from his work cafeteria.

He bet Rebekah's fridge was full of healthy meals she'd already prepared earlier in the week and then labeled in containers with color-coded lids. He opened the beer and was swallowing the first frothy gulp when his phone lit up with her response.

He's kind of handsome.

Kind of. Kicking off his sneakers, he took another drink and opened the doors leading out to his twelfth-floor balcony. He could get her to do better than that.

Kind of incredibly handsome. Your kids are going to be gorgeous. Hopefully with your dimples and his surfing skills. Plus, they'll be smart.

Surfing, questionable (and only if it's in shallow water). Dimples, maybe. Smart, probably. But that'll also be from me.

Obviously, he wrote. So do you and this kind of incredibly handsome Grant with the amazing surfing skills plan to raise your children together?

I'm not sure how that'll work. Hopefully, my parents aren't going to ask for those kind of details.

Well, the role-playing gig had been good while it lasted.

Don't you think they'll have questions about our relationship, Rebekah? Like how long we've known each other. Whether we plan to get married. Things like that?

Again, she didn't reply right away and Grant ran a hand through his hair and looked at the waves crashing on the beach below. His phone finally buzzed. But this time, it wasn't a text. She was actually calling him. He nearly dropped the phone as he scrambled to slide his thumb across the screen and answer. "Hello?"

"I honestly don't know what to tell them," she admitted, not bothering with a greeting.

"There's always the truth."

"Grant, I can't tell my parents that I had a one-night stand with my bosses' nephew."

"Do you think they'd disown you or something? Your parents seemed pretty reasonable and progressive to me."

"Obviously, I *can* tell them. I just don't *want* to. I'm their only child, the apple of their eye. High school valedictorian and top of my class at Duke's School of Business. I love my parents and they love me, but you know how they used to foster all those babies? Well, that took up a lot of their time and energy when I was a child. They've always counted on me to be responsible and self-reliant and, well, now they're used to me always doing things right. I'm not the type of person who makes mistakes."

Ouch. Was she calling him the mistake? Or their children the mistake? He pinched the bridge of his nose and said, "So then don't tell them it was a one-night stand. I mean, you heard your dad earlier today. He already referred to you as my girlfriend."

"Because that's what you told him on the plane." The reminder still held a trace of accusation and Grant could feel the defensiveness building in his throat.

"Yet again, I had no idea that was your father. Besides, you weren't exactly blowing up my phone with conversations and I had to talk to someone about it."

She made a huffing sound, then grumbled through the receiver. "Well, I'm talking to you about it now."

"So going back to my suggestion earlier. Why not just let people think we're dating each other? Or do I embarrass you?" He wasn't exactly a player, but he'd never really had to work too hard at attracting women. At least, he hadn't until he met Rebekah. He held his breath as he awaited her response.

"Fine." This time he heard her actual sigh and a current of electricity shot through him. "We can pretend we're dating each other."

"Can I pretend to take you out to dinner when I come into town next week?" he asked.

"It depends on what your definition of *pretend* is."

"Oh, you know, the usual. I pick you up at your place and hold the doors open for you. Maybe you smile at me and laugh at my jokes as though you enjoy my company."

"I've smiled at you before, Grant."

"Only when you've had a couple of cocktails, which are now apparently off-limits according to my baby book."

"I know. So is coffee, unfortunately."

"So you'll have to be sober and uncaffeinated and smile at me anyway," he added. "Possibly even hold my hand. I'd also be more than willing to engage in some public kissing displays, if you think it'll make us seem more legitimate."

"And you're hoping that people will actually see us? That a dinner with some hand-holding—no public kissing displays—will convince them that we're boyfriend and girlfriend?"

"They will if we go somewhere romantic. Not, like, too romantic because that would seem like we're trying too hard. But maybe a nice place that requires you to wear the green, silky top you had on that night at happy hour. The one with the V-neck that showed off the magnificent view of your—"

"Grant." Her voice came out in a squeak and she cleared her throat. "I don't know if this kind of pretending is such a good idea."

"Trust me. I'm in marketing and can make anything look believable. Besides, what could go wrong?"

"I should've told him that a million things could go wrong," Rebekah said to the hole under the front porch of the old brick house the following Thursday. She still had no idea whether the scruffy gray dog was currently hiding under there, but every day she'd been stopping by on her way to work and *something* had been eating the specialty canine cookies she'd been adding to her usual order at the bakery.

"Grant Whitaker is like this flaky, buttery croissant right here. I know he'll end up being bad for me, but I can't seem to resist him." She bit down, letting the layers of pastry melt into her mouth as she tried not to think about all the extra calories. Swallowing, she added, "It's just that he'd been talking about my dimples and my cleavage and saying all these other flirty things that kept distracting me. My brain was flashing the warning lights, but my heart was bouncing around inside my chest and my hormones were going crazy, which is supposedly normal according to the research I've been doing. So, yeah, I guess that's how Grant convinced me that we should pretend we're boyfriend and girlfriend."

A truck drove by slowly and Rebekah prayed the driver didn't notice the crazy pregnant woman sitting outside of a house that didn't belong to her and talking to an elusive stray animal that probably wished she'd just shut up and leave it alone. Or maybe find a human to whine to, instead.

Sure, Rebekah had several girlfriends who lived in town, but most of them either volunteered at the animal shelter or were somehow connected to someone who worked there. So it wasn't like she could talk to them about what was going on between herself and Grant. At least, not yet.

"So I finally bit the bullet and called my parents last night," Rebekah continued after a few more cars passed. "They pretty much asked me every question that Grant and I had already practiced. But I felt like the biggest fraud on the planet when I told them that Grant and I had been seeing each other for a while. Anyone who knows me will realize that he's totally not my type. He's all laid-back and I'm more of a type A personality. He has all these big, bold pie-in-the-sky ideas and I'm a realist. Everyone'll see through this whole stupid fake relationship idea that he thinks is foolproof. And you know who's going to look like the biggest fool in all of this?"

Not that Rebekah expected the dog to answer, but the question gave her time to take a sip of her decaf latte. "Me. I'm going to get swept up in all his flirty banter and his sexy smiles, and before you know it, even *I'll* start believing that our relationship is legit. Do you know what he told me when we were on the phone? He said he was in marketing and could make anything look believable. I mean, the guy might as well have said that he tells lies for a living. And this is the man I'm supposed to trust? Who I'm supposed to raise kids with?"

A rustling sound came from under the porch and Rebekah held herself perfectly still as her excitement spiked. She had to remain calm and keep talking if she wanted the dog to feel safe enough to come out from its hiding spot. Staring intently at the hole as though she could will the mutt to do her bidding, she dropped a small piece of the canine cookie. "You and I are a lot alike, you know. We both have trust issues, obviously, and prefer to keep to ourselves. We both like baked goods and bacon on our cheeseburgers and hanging around old front porches of houses that don't belong to us."

"You smell a whole helluva lot better than that dog, though," Grant said as he walked up the rutted driveway.

Rebekah scrambled to her feet, heat radiating from her cheeks. "What are you doing here?"

"I always stop by here when I'm in town to check on our friend." Grant held up a fast-food bag. "I was hoping a sausage biscuit might do the trick to lure him out today."

Just when Rebekah had herself convinced that Grant was all kinds of wrong for her, he showed up out of nowhere, doing something sweet and thoughtful to make her completely rethink her entire opinion of the man. Like feeding a stray dog, or refereeing a schoolgirl argument about unicorns and dinosaurs, or asking a stranger on an airplane for tips on the best way to soothe a crying baby—her dad hadn't stopped talking about Grant's earnest commitment to being a good father.

She commanded her nerve endings to settle down

and pushed a few curls behind her ear. "I meant why are you in town? I thought you weren't coming until this weekend."

Their plan had been to go out in public together a few times here and there, then maybe next month he could stop by her office and take her out to lunch. Once people were used to seeing them together, then they'd tell everyone about the babies. But his showing up out of the blue like this wasn't sticking to the plan. Even if it was only a day ahead of schedule.

"Oh, Aunt Bunny has it her head that we should build some sort of aviary on the premises and wants me to go with her to check out this bird sanctuary near the Outer Banks. I'm going to use the drive to try to convince her that they're not running an actual zoo here in Spring Forest."

"Oh. Okay. Well, I guess I'd better get to the office." She grabbed her bag and her decaf latte off the porch steps.

Grant's gaze traveled the length of her body and every inch of her skin zapped with electricity as his eyes passed over her. Finally, he lifted his face to hers and asked, "What? No kiss hello for your boyfriend?"

Rebekah's mouth went dry and her knees gave a little wobble. "Um…here? There's no one around to even see us. It'd be like putting on a show with no audience."

"Yeah, but when it's curtain time, we're going to want our performance to look as real as possible." Grant lifted one of his broad shoulders in a shrug. "We can consider it a dress rehearsal."

He moved in closer and Rebekah's breath caught in her throat. Her tummy did a little cartwheel and she immediately moved her hand to her midsection. "Don't you think we've already had enough practice?"

His head lowered to the slight rounding just below her waist. It was probably only noticeable to her, but she'd purposely worn an A-line skirt this morning to make it less apparent and to buy herself a little more time before everyone noticed.

Instead of looking suitably chastised, the man lifted one side of his mouth into a satisfied smile. He took another step closer. His fingers reached up to a curl that had blown into her face, gently toying with it before pushing it behind her ear to join the others. "In that case, I'll follow you to the animal shelter and then we can actually get the show on the road."

Rebekah's knees gave more than a wobble as she hurried to her car. If he kept looking at her with those steamy blue eyes, nobody was going to think her physical reaction to Grant was just an act.

Chapter Eight

It wasn't until Rebekah was a mile down the road that she realized she'd forgotten to leave the rest of the canine cookie for the gray dog.

"Our friend," Grant had called it. She could turn around and go back, but that might make it seem to Grant as though she was stalling for time to avoid being seen with her pretend boyfriend, who was also the very real father of her children.

Seeing his rental car in her rearview mirror, she realized that she probably should've taken him up on his offer of a dress rehearsal. If they'd just kissed and gotten it over with, then she wouldn't have all this awkward anticipation rioting around inside of her right this second.

When they did pull into the parking lot at Furever Paws, there was so much activity going on Rebekah wanted to keep driving. But everyone had probably already seen her unmistakable car and Grant's plain white rental sedan.

The sign guys were back and installing the newly reworded sign with the shelter's full name. Bobby Doyle, the mechanic who'd built the small bleachers for what was now being called the Learning Center, was under the hood of the older van they used to transport animals. Plus, there was a small bus from the Senior Center unloading volunteers who called themselves the Snuggle Crew.

The only blessing was that Bunny and Birdie were nowhere in sight when Grant exited his car and walked over to her driver's-side door. Rebekah knew that this might be her only chance to have the upper hand and so she rose to her full five feet nine inches and tried to sound as casual as possible when she said, "Oh, hey, Grant. What a surprise to see you here."

Without checking to see if their audience was even paying attention, Rebekah gave him a quick peck on his cheek. He must not have been anticipating it, because he stood there rooted to the spot, despite the fact that her tote bag accidentally bounced off his hip as she tried to hustle past, pretending her lips weren't still tingling from where they'd pressed against his golden stubble.

When he caught up to her near the front entrance, he pulled open one of the glass doors and said under his breath, "I think our kisses hello could definitely use more practice, Taylor."

With the way he'd used her last name, as if they were some sort of teammates, she was half expecting him to give her a smack on the butt like they were coming out of a football huddle. Instead of being offended, though, a tiny thrill shot through her. They *were* on the same team and, for the first time, it wasn't based solely on their mutual attraction. She and Grant were actually partners in something that was bigger than both of them.

Her eyes dropped to his lips and her heartbeat pounded in her chest. "I guess a little more practice wouldn't hurt."

"There you are," Nancy said from behind the reception desk and Rebekah felt the heat rise to her cheeks. She'd been about to kiss Grant, right here in front of everyone at work. What had she been thinking?

Walking on unsteady legs, Rebekah realized Claire Asher was also standing near the reception desk.

"Hey, Claire," Rebekah greeted her friend, hoping the woman didn't notice that her voice was still a bit breathless. "Isn't it a school day?"

"It is, but most of my English students are on a field trip with their eighth-grade science teachers." Claire smiled and pointed to her fiancé, Matt Fielding, who was standing nearby in the lobby and talking to one of the senior citizen volunteers. This particular man was wearing a blue cap embroidered with the words Vietnam Veteran. "Matt convinced me to call in a substitute so we could get a jump start on the wedding planning."

"Have you guys set a date yet?" Rebekah was happy for the engaged couple who were also renovating a fixer-upper they'd recently purchased, but she wasn't sure why they'd come to an animal rescue when they should be out sampling cake flavors.

"We're thinking around Christmastime. In fact, I was talking to Nancy the other day about taking on a couple more fosters now that we've got our yard finished and she mentioned that Furever Paws was going to be throwing some sort of fund-raiser gala soon. She said we should come by and check out the new party pavilion you guys were working on. So here we are."

"What party pavilion?" Rebekah tilted her head as she looked at Nancy.

"Isn't that what you called it in your brochures, Grant?" the middle-aged foster coordinator asked, reminding Rebekah that her supposed boyfriend was right behind her.

"Everyone kept referring to it as the picnic area," he said, placing his hand on Rebekah's lower back. The heat from his palm was immediately noticeable and caused an unexpected shiver as he slid it to the opposite side of her waist. "But I figured that once we get the freestanding roof built, it'll be well suited to hosting parties and should have a catchier name. It's also technically on Whitaker Acres, which is private land, so it shouldn't affect the nonprofit's tax exemption status."

Of course Grant had come up with yet another solution to an issue Rebekah had tried not to think about. She should be grateful, but instead she saw the boundaries between them growing even fuzzier.

A phone rang down the hall and she shifted her tote bag to her other shoulder, thereby dislodging Grant's arm from around her waist. "I really need to get to my office and take that call. Grant, why don't you show

Matt and Claire your so-called party pavilion for their upcoming wedding?"

Let her friend Claire be the one to point out to the guy from Florida that it often snowed in Spring Forest during December. How practical would his fancified outdoor picnic area be then?

"Well, I'm not exactly a wedding planner…" he started and Rebekah raised one eyebrow as though to say, *you're not exactly my boyfriend, either, but you have no problem using your marketing skills to play pretend when it suits you.* He must've understood her look because he finished with, "But I'm happy to show you guys around."

She rolled her eyes and was halfway down the hall when Grant's voice stopped her. "Hey, Rebekah, let me know what time you want to go grab lunch."

Grant had never wanted to kiss a woman more than he had when he'd seen Rebekah sitting outside that old mansion this morning, talking to a stray animal that refused to come out of its hiding spot.

He'd surprised her by showing up today instead of tomorrow like they'd planned. He'd also surprised her by putting his arm around her when she was standing in the middle of the lobby for all the shelter volunteers to see. The thin, silky material of her top wasn't much of a barrier between his palm and her heated skin underneath, and he'd ended up being the one surprised by his physical reaction to her.

Which was why he'd made that parting shot in front of everyone about taking her out to lunch. He'd needed to feel as though he hadn't totally lost control where she was concerned. In fact, when the poised and proper Rebekah Taylor was thrown off her game, it provided Grant the opportunity to come in and save the day.

And he'd always been good at saving the day.

"You ready?" he asked as he walked into Rebekah's office at noon.

She kept her eyes on her computer screen and her fingers on her keyboard as she spoke. "Ready for what?"

"For lunch. I was thinking Main Street Grille, but we can go somewhere more romantic if you really want to put on a show."

Her head slowly swiveled toward where he stood, and despite the fact that she was still in her desk chair, she appeared to be looking down at him. "Fine. Main Street Grille, but for lunch only. No show."

He lifted his right palm as though he was taking an oath. "I promise to keep my hands to myself. Unless you beg me to put them on you. Like you did that night—"

"Grant!" she yelped, which made him laugh. The only thing better than surprising Rebekah was shocking her.

Several heads turned in their direction as Grant kept pace with her long-legged stride toward the exit. After their near kiss on the way in earlier, everyone would be talking about them before they even made it out of the parking lot. His chest instinctively expanded as he held the door for her.

Yep, their fake relationship was off and running.

Speaking of running, they were halfway to his rental car when he saw a gray flash in the distance.

"Hold on." He grabbed her elbow and she shot him a frown before giving a pointed look at where he was touching her.

"Is this your way of keeping your hands to yourself?" she asked.

"No, look over there." The gray dog was under one of the bushes near her little blue Fiat, its beady black eyes watching them. He felt Rebekah's muscles tense under his fingers.

"I have a treat for him in my car," she whispered to him. "I'm going to slowly walk over there and open the passenger door. Stay here and don't make eye contact."

The Furever Paws van was still in its parking spot where Bobby had been working on it, which meant Grant could turn his head in the other direction and watch Rebekah in the reflection of the rear window. His pulse thrummed in his ears as her high heels crunched against the gravel. After at least a million seconds, the door handle finally made a clicking sound.

As Rebekah slowly retreated from the car, her eyes met his in the reflection from the van window and she paused a few feet away from her Fiat, her back to the dog.

They held their positions for what felt like forever but was probably only a few minutes. Grant could smell the dog well before he saw it approach the car. The scruffy mutt hopped up on the passenger seat and, when its nose was buried in the white paper bakery bag, Rebekah ran the few feet and slammed the door closed.

Without a backward glance, she raced toward the front entrance of the building.

She was already inside when the gray dog pressed its paws against her passenger window and began barking for all it was worth. The animal's frightened eyes narrowed as Grant walked closer to the car, trying to murmur words that would calm the poor thing down.

"You're okay, buddy. We just want to help, that's all."

The dog's barking subsided for a second and Grant thought he was making progress, but then Davis McIntyre, the on-duty vet tech, came outside with a lead pole and a small metal kennel. Lauren Jackson, the veterinarian who had taken over her father's veterinary practice, followed. Judging by the way the small dog was growling and baring its teeth, Grant wanted to call out the suggestion that they bring a tranquilizer gun, too.

One of the volunteer dog handlers emerged from the shelter's doors wearing long, thick gloves made out of suede and it was then that he caught a glimpse of Rebekah standing behind the door of the building. Was she afraid of the dog? Or maybe she was worried about getting bitten by a feral animal and she wanted to protect the babies.

There was lots of barking and growling and *whoa theres* but they finally got the poor little beast out of the car and into the crate. That was when Rebekah flew through the doors and grabbed Grant's arm. "Is he okay?"

"Judging by all the commotion he's making, I'd say he's mad as hell. But they've got him."

Rebekah's palm slid down his arm and into his hand, her fingers lacing with his as they followed everyone inside to the exam area in the rear of the building. When they set the crate on a stainless steel table, the dog's barking picked up speed, a scared animal who knew there was no getting away but wasn't going down without a fight.

"I'm going to have to sedate him so I can perform the examination," Dr. Lauren said, opening a package that contained a syringe. There was more growling and the crate shuddered but the vet and vet tech blocked their view.

Gradually the barking grew intermittent and that's when Rebekah finally approached. "It's okay, buddy. You're going to be okay."

She held out her fingers and the overgrown gray muzzle nuzzled against the metal bars as though it wanted to rub up against her hand. "That's a good boy." Rebekah looked toward Dr. Lauren. "He's a boy, right?"

"I only got a quick glance, but it looked that way to me," the vet said as she laid out supplies on the tray near the table.

"You remember me, don't you?" Rebekah asked the animal who was now lying on his side, his barking subdued but his eyes still very wary. "I'm the one bringing you all those good treats all the time."

A little pink tongue poked out of the mass of gray fur and licked Rebekah's fingers. "That's a good boy. Now, these nice people just want to check you out and make sure you don't have any ouchies. Then when you feel better, I'll have another treat for you."

"Ouchies?" Grant asked when Rebekah finally backed away from the now-peaceful dog and let the vet go to work.

"Sorry. It's something my parents used to say when I was little. With all the stress, I guess it slipped out."

"Is that why you stayed inside when they were trying to get the dog out of your car?" Wanting to check her heart rate, he used his thumb to trace the pulse point on her wrist. "Was it too much stress?"

"No, I was hiding because I didn't want him to see me and think I was the one who trapped him."

"So you were leaving me out there to be the bad guy and take the fall?"

"As if anyone could ever think that Grant Whitaker is the bad guy."

"What's that supposed to mean?" he asked, but then Davis appeared in the doorway holding an extra chair.

"Since both of you don't seem to want to go anywhere, you can just sit over here where you'll be out of the way." Davis was great with animals but had never seemed especially fond of humans.

"Is April Oliver around?" Dr. Lauren asked, referring to the professional groomer who often volunteered at the shelter. "The hair around his ears is so matted, I can't even lift them. We might need her to groom him before I can get in there and really examine him."

"I have a feeling this might take a while," Grant told Rebekah. "Are you hungry?"

"I don't think I should leave. When I was talking to him a few minutes ago, it seemed like he knew my voice and it helped relax him."

Or it could be the sedation doing the relaxing, but Grant admired her for wanting to stay by the dog's side. She might not be excited about her pregnancy but judging by the concern etched all over her face for some stray animal, she was going to make one hell of a mother.

"Despite being on the thin side, he's relatively healthy," Dr. Lauren told Rebekah over an hour later. "Poor guy was probably in a ton of pain, though, with all that matted hair pulling on his skin and the flea bites underneath. The hair inside his ears was so bad, it had grown into these waxy dreadlock things that were harder to remove than a cork out of a champagne bottle. There's an infection in both canals, but I was able to flush them out and we'll get him started on some antibiotics."

"He already looks like a completely different animal," Rebekah said, stroking her hand against the soft gray fur that had been shaved down to half an inch of fuzz. April had been able to carefully bathe him earlier and he smelled like a whole new dog, as well.

"Be cautious, though. When he wakes up, he might be just as grouchy as he was before we sedated him."

Grant had gone to get sandwiches for them and Rebekah had only been able to get down a few bites. She'd been on the edge of her seat the whole time the groomer and then the vet had been working on the dog.

"We got a hit on his microchip." Birdie waved a piece of paper in the air as she came into the exam room with Doc J behind her. "Two-and-a-half-year-old schnauzer and terrier mix named Angus. He belonged to Rupert MacKenzie, who used to live at 436 Second Avenue. But Rupert went into a skilled nursing facility after he had a stroke over a year ago. He passed away after a few months with no known relatives and the house is now tied up in probate."

"That explains why the little guy was hiding under the porch over there," Grant said, his large, tan hand following Rebekah's as he petted the still-sleeping animal. "You were looking for your owner, huh, Angus MacKenzie? Wow, that's a proud Scottish name if I ever heard one."

"He's probably got some Scottie in him," Doc J added, as he looked over his daughter's patient. The man was supposed to be retired, but he sure stopped by an awful lot to check on things. "They can be pretty independent and stubborn, so that's why he was so determined to stay close to home."

The dog let out a big breath and his eyelids fluttered open. His gray bangs had been cut back, allowing him to see better. Although now they stood up straight, as though his brow was lifted in a permanent state of annoyance. Rebekah felt the vibration in his chest as he started to growl. "You're okay. Take it easy. As soon as Dr. Lauren says it's okay, I'll get you something to eat."

His freshly trimmed ears lifted in surprise and his little nub of a tail began to wag in earnest. An encouraging smile spread across Rebekah's face. "Do you recognize the sound of my voice, Angus?"

The dog's tail wagged even more and he sniffed Rebekah's hand before licking it. "He's probably just excited to hear anyone's voice at this point," Dr. Lauren said as she put the oxygen mask away. "As bad as his ears were, he probably couldn't hear a lot for the past few months. It certainly explains why he was so afraid of everyone and kept running off."

That might be true, but despite all the people in the room, Angus's round black eyes were focused on Rebekah. Sure, she'd been having in-depth conversations with the animal for over a week now, as though he was her personal therapist. However, there was something else pulling at Rebekah's heart as she slowly stroked the area between his ears and down his neck. Some unexplainable connection that drew her to this dog.

"I'm going to try and take the lead off," Dr. Lauren advised them. "April found this green plaid collar that looks pretty fitting for our little chieftain here."

Rebekah took a step back to give the vet room to work, but Angus made a whining sound.

"He seems to prefer you," Grant told her. "Maybe you should put the collar on."

Dr. Lauren passed her the collar and Rebekah slowly put it around Angus's neck. The last thing she wanted to do was startle the poor guy and get him agitated again. As soon as the plastic clasp clicked into place, the dog rose onto his four legs and used his nose to nuzzle into her hands.

"Look at that tail." Grant gave her a smile of encouragement before chuckling. "It's wagging so hard, his whole rear end is shaking along with it."

"So how long do we need to keep him under observation?" Birdie asked the younger vet. "We're pretty full right now and I'd really hate to put him in one of our temporary kennels after all the earlier trauma he endured this morning. They might remind him of a cage and stress him out again."

"I'd keep an eye on him for another hour or so, but he should be good to go if you can line up a foster home tonight."

"Do you hear that, Angus?" Rebekah murmured as the dog cuddled against her, burrowing himself into her arms until she was practically carrying him like a baby. "You get to go to a foster home tonight where someone will love on you and take care of you and feed you yummy treats..."

Her voice trailed off as she realized that every eye in the room was on her.

"What?" Rebekah narrowed her eyes at Grant, because his knowing grin was the most unsettling.

"I'm pretty sure that the only home Angus is going to be happy with is yours."

"But I don't foster dogs. Or any pets." Rebekah could see that her protests were falling on deaf ears. Which reminded her that while the little gray bundle of fur had recently been partially deaf, he could probably hear her *now* as she was telling everyone that she didn't want him. "It's just that my place isn't really set up for a pet. I don't even have a food dish or any supplies."

"Honey, we're an animal shelter." Birdie shook her head. "We have everything you could possibly need. I'll even let you pick out some new stuff from the gift shop out front."

Angus's soul-searching black eyes didn't so much as blink as he stared at her adoringly.

"That's it, Angus." Grant scratched the dog's lower

back and Rebekah could've sworn she felt the thing purr along with the man's playful tone. "Keep giving her that sad puppy-dog look and guilt her into taking you home with her."

But Angus didn't need any coaching. He was already as good as Grant when it came to wearing down her sense of logic.

Rebekah's heart hammered. This was all happening way too fast. She needed to think of a way to get out of it. "What if that sad look is really just the aftereffects of the sedation? What if I get him home and he gets all worked up again?"

"That's a good point." Grant kept his eyes on her when he told the others in the room, "We really wouldn't want to put Rebekah in a situation that could risk the… could risk her health."

She lowered her lids at him in warning, but he only lifted his brows and shrugged at her in response. If she hadn't been so busy trying to silently communicate with him, she might've seen his aunt studying their interaction.

That's why Rebekah choked back a gasp when Birdie suggested, "Why don't you take Grant with you and Angus back to your place? That way, if the dog seems like he's going to turn on you, you won't be on your own."

Damn it. Rebekah was supposed to be getting herself *out* of this foster-dog commitment, not digging herself in deeper. Now she was supposed to be taking both the dog *and* Grant to her house?

"But what do I do with him tomorrow?" she countered. "I work all day and wouldn't really be able to watch him."

"I was actually going to talk to you about your schedule." Her boss shifted forward and Rebekah saw something in the older woman's eyes. "Bunny was supposed to go to the bird sanctuary with Grant today, but then you guys got busy with Angus here. Since she's busy tomorrow, I'm going to need you to go with Grant to the bird place. You can take Angus here with you and see how he does with cars rides and leashes. If that goes well, maybe take him to a park to socialize him with other people and animals. We need to know if he'll need some training classes with Mollie before we can officially adopt him out."

She opened her mouth to attempt one last stand. But Birdie and Doc J were already walking away. Besides, at this point, any further arguments would clearly only result in Rebekah landing herself in an even deeper hole she would not be able to dig her way out of.

"Fine," she mumbled, then patted the dog's chest. "But you two had better not get me into any trouble."

Angus made a contented sigh and Grant was looking anywhere but at Rebekah. Although she couldn't help but note his lips were twitching at the corners.

Chapter Nine

"**S**orry for throwing off your plans with your aunt today," Rebekah said to Grant as he drove her and Angus to her townhome. She'd left her car back at the shelter so she could hold Angus in case he needed to be soothed during the ride. "I didn't intend for you to miss out on your trip to the Outer Banks with Bunny."

Now that the chaos of the afternoon had receded, he could sense her slipping back into her perfectly composed self. Or, at least, she was making a brave effort. But Grant could still feel the imprint of her fingers from where she'd clung to his hand while the animal was being examined.

"I figured you and Angus needed me more." Grant smiled across the center console, reaching to pet the dog who was currently balanced on Rebekah's lap and had his snout halfway out the window. "Isn't that right, big guy?"

Angus turned his face toward Grant, giving him a cautious appraisal before looking back out the window. He sure was a cute little thing now that he'd been cleaned up.

"To be honest, this kind of works out better anyway," he offered.

"How so?" Rebekah changed her grip on the plaid leash that matched the dog's collar, probably because she was worried the pup was going to make another break for it through the open window.

Grant held back a chuckle. As much as she'd argued against fostering the abandoned animal, everyone in that room could see the connection between her and the dog. It was going to be interesting to watch how she and Angus interacted once he got them back to her place.

"Now we have even more reason to spend time together and get people thinking that things are serious between us." He felt the corners of his mouth lift in a smug grin.

"Serious between us? I thought we were just pretending to be boyfriend and girlfriend, remember? Why do you always have to take things to the next level?"

"Always?" he repeated, his bold wink hidden behind the dark lens of his sunglasses. If Rebekah was arguing with him, it meant she was back to feeling like herself. Since his current goal was keeping her as stress-free as possible, he'd gladly engage in a spirited debate to distract her from worrying about her new foster dog. "What else do I take to the next level?"

Her curls were blowing around in the wind from the open window and she groaned as she tried to use her free hand to hold them back. "How about that party pavilion, for starters?"

"So I took a few liberties with the name. But you have to admit that it has a nice ring to it."

"The problem is that we're running an animal shelter, Grant. Not an events venue."

"But it's an animal shelter that's barely making ends meet. I would think that with your business background, you'd see my aunts desperately need to be bringing in more revenue."

"They wouldn't need to bring in more revenue if..." Rebekah's words trailed off.

"If what?"

She sighed. "It's no secret that there's an investigation right now into what happened to their investment money."

Sure, he was hoping that the attorney investigating the matter would get to the bottom of the matter, but he was also hoping that Uncle Gator would be cleared of any wrongdoing in the process.

"Have you been updated on that investigation lately?" she asked.

"No, because I don't want to deal with theories or what-ifs. I want hard, concrete proof of whoever could possibly be behind their current money mismanagement."

Rebekah lifted a finger. "Nope. Not *current* mismanagement. As their office director, who is solely responsible for the budget, I can assure you that that all their financial issues happened well before I was ever hired. So you can quit giving me the side-eye."

"What side-eye?" He lifted his sunglasses to the top of his head and squinted in her direction.

"The one you're giving me right now." She reached up to the rearview mirror and lowered it to reflect his suspicious expression. "You've been looking at me like that for the past year, as though you think I'm hiding something."

"I don't necessarily think you're hiding something. I just have a feeling that there's another side to you. One that I've only gotten glimpses of so far. Plus, I'm trying to stay focused and resist the urge to stare at your long, pretty legs."

He could hear her intake of breath and tried not to laugh as she attempted to tug the hem of her dress down past her knees. Too bad she couldn't move it past Angus's squirmy hind end.

"Why do you do that?" he asked.

"Do what?"

"Get all embarrassed whenever I pay you a compliment."

"I'm not embarrassed." Rebekah defended herself even as she shifted in her seat and seemed fixated on the billboard advertising the new Kingdom Creek development. The same billboard she probably passed every single day on her way home from work. "It's just weird, that's all."

"Me being attracted to you is weird?" He had to say it out loud to make sure he understood her.

"No, you being attracted to your aunts' employee is weird."

"It has nothing to do with you working for my family. Even if you were the employee of an entire herd of feral Uni-rexes trying to take over the planet, I'd still be attracted to you."

Rebekah pointed at the road ahead. "Go right at the next light."

"I know it's been a couple of months, but I remember how to get to your townhouse." He saw her cheeks suck in as she inhaled and it stirred his blood. He added, "In fact, I remember a lot of things about that night."

Angus again yipped in excitement and she covered the dog's floppy ears. "Don't talk about...*you know*... in front of the dog."

"I doubt he can understand what we're saying." Grant nodded at the animal who was currently using his open mouth and tongue to try and catch the air rushing by the open window.

Rebekah frowned. "I know it sounds crazy, but I'm pretty sure he knows *exactly* what's being said."

"Well, then, he's going to find out sooner or later that his new mommy is going to be a mommy to some humans pretty soon."

"I wish you wouldn't call me that."

Grant cocked his head at her while they waited at the stop sign in front of her complex. "You don't want our kids to call you mommy?"

"No, I don't want the d-o-g to start thinking of me that way." She'd lowered her voice to spell the word. "This is only a temporary fostering situation."

Ten minutes later, after Angus had left his mark on every shrub and patch of grass along the walk from the parking lot to her unit, the so-called d-o-g was curled up in the center of her white leather sofa as though it was his throne. Grant chuckled as he filled up the new water dish. "Looks like our Scottish warrior has laid claim to the castle and has no intention of this being a temporary situation."

"But I don't really want the responsibility of a pet," Rebekah whispered as she filled the equally new ceramic bone-shaped storage canister with dog treats. "Especially right now with everything else going on."

"Sometimes we don't get to pick our pets." Grant shrugged. "Sometimes our pets pick us."

"Do you have any pets back home?" Rebekah leaned against the kitchen counter across from him. It was one of those questions that would've come up already if they'd gone on any proper dates. Or had been in an actual relationship and not just pretending.

"I always had a dog growing up, but now I travel too much to take care of one." He put his hands on the counter behind him and rolled back his shoulders in an attempt to stretch his upper torso. "My mom has a corgi, though, and I get my animal fix whenever I visit her surf shop. Or, obviously, when I come see my aunts."

"Which you've been doing with increased frequency lately." Her eyes lowered to his chest, which he knew was on full display under the very thin cotton of his T-shirt. Her tongue darted out of her mouth to lick her lips and then her gaze jumped back up to his face. "Not that I've noticed or anything."

Too late, he thought, flexing his pec muscles. Rebekah's earlier admission, as well as the unresolved sexual tension, hung in the air between them.

"Well, you'd better get used to it, because now that I'm going to be a father, I'll be here an awful lot more." Okay, so Grant hadn't really thought much about the logistics of living so far away while still being there to support Rebekah through the pregnancy and parenthood, but as soon as he'd said the words, he realized that he couldn't keep up with the back-and-forth travel indefinitely. Something would have to give.

"What about your job?" Rebekah turned to open the refrigerator and pulled out two bottles of water, handing him one. His fingers grazed hers and he was reminded of how her hand had clung to his most of this afternoon while Angus had been under sedation.

Despite her attempt to avoid his gaze, Grant was willing to wager that she'd just remembered the same thing. In fact, he saw her fingers twitch slightly before she drew them back, gripping the counter behind her as though she were holding herself in place. She shook her head and he caught a whiff of her plumeria scent and inhaled deeply.

"One nice thing about my job is that I can work from pretty much anywhere." He twisted off the water bottle's cap and took a long drink. When he lowered his head, he caught her staring at his neck.

A current of electricity shot through him and when she licked her lips a second time, Grant took a step closer. He didn't know if it was desire or courage currently flooding his body, but he'd grown extremely warm and he needed Rebekah to understand that he could only take so much heat before he needed to get out of this kitchen.

"Rebekah?" Her name came out in a near groan.

"Huh?" she said, giving her head another little shake before lifting it to face him.

"You know how you told me in the car that I'm always looking at you with a side-eye?" He took another step closer.

"Uh-huh," she managed as her eyes darted down to his mouth.

"And I told you that I stare at you because I'm attracted to you?"

She sucked in her cheeks and gave a brief nod.

"Well, you have a tendency to watch me in the exact same way." She was still wearing her heels, making her nearly the same height as him. Which meant that his face was within inches of hers.

"What do you mean?" Her whisper-soft answer was so close, he could feel the ice-water coolness of her breath against his mouth.

"It means that if you keep looking at me like that, we're going to end up in your bedroom again."

One minute Rebekah had been in the kitchen guzzling cold water in an attempt to cool down the throbbing of awareness heating her blood. And the next she was kicking off her wedged heels as Grant led her backward toward her bed. His lips were just as warm and as fierce as she remembered and his mouth consumed hers while she lifted up his T-shirt to stroke the golden skin underneath.

"Are you sure?" he asked when they were nearly to her bed.

Lately, it seemed as if everything was being decided for her—unexpected twins, foster dogs, party pavilions. But her body was still the one thing she controlled. And she was absolutely sure that she wanted just one more night with Grant—one night to really get it right.

Not that alcohol had totally impaired them last time, but she was more than sober right this second and needed to prove to herself, and maybe even to him, that whatever it was between them wasn't really a big deal.

However, when she finally got his shirt over his head and those perfectly broad shoulders were in full view, all she could think was, *This is a very big, very muscular deal.*

How could one man be this incredibly handsome? Or smell this good? She knew he'd been on a plane and then at the animal shelter all day, yet his skin still held traces of coconut-scented sunscreen. Rebekah would've used her tongue to taste him; however, her mouth was currently occupied by his deep, exploring kisses.

She slid her palms over the wall that was his chest, then over the smooth ridges of his abdomen until she got to the muscular lines that dipped into his board shorts. Her heart sped up when she got to his waistband, yet her hands slowed down. If this was going to be the last time she allowed herself to sleep with the man, then she was going to take her time.

Grant, though, must've mistaken her pause as a request for assistance because his hands encircled hers at his waist and then she heard Velcro rip as he released the fastening. Rebekah was about to have sex with a man for a second time and she didn't even know if he owned a proper pair of pants.

When he stood before her completely naked, his casual clothing preferences suddenly didn't matter. Rebekah gulped, unable to take her hands off him.

Or her eyes.

She didn't want to ruin the moment with logical thoughts about him eventually flying out of her life for good. So she looked her fill, instead, memorizing every perfect muscle forged by years of swimming and surfing.

"Now my turn," he said, his fingers making their way to the zipper on the back of her dress. As the coolness from her air-conditioning unit hit the bare skin along her lower spine, Rebekah suddenly had the urge to pull her dress closed. She'd always been on the curvier side, but her stomach was even less flat than it had been a couple of months ago. Or even a couple of weeks ago.

Then his hands were on her breasts and Rebekah forgot every single thing she'd been thinking up until that point. Throwing her head back, she let out a moan and Grant pressed his lips to her jawline and then trailed kisses down her neck and along her shoulder blades.

She whimpered when he removed his hands from the sharpened peaks of her nipples, which were now aching for more. "Be patient, sweetheart," he murmured in her ear. "As sexy as this purple silky bra is, I need it out of my way so I can feel all of you."

When she was finally standing bare in front of him, it was Grant who groaned as he reached out and gently stroked her breasts. "I've been thinking about your body for months, thinking about all the ways I'd like to touch you and make you feel—"

He wasn't able to finish because she captured his face between her hands and pulled his mouth back to hers. Months, he'd said. Knowing that all this time Grant had been thinking about her body the way she'd been thinking about his made Rebekah nearly drunk with power.

He tilted his head and deepened the kiss while maneuvering the matching panties over her hips. After she kicked them free, he hooked his right wrist under her left knee and she could easily feel his arousal at her opening. The hard length of him slid against her and Rebekah wondered if Grant planned to take her right there, standing up. She arched her hips toward him and he drew back. "I brought protection along this time, but it's in my carry-on bag. Which is outside in my car."

"At the risk of killing the mood," Rebekah replied, her voice sounding raspy to her own ears. "Unless you have some test results you need to share with me, I think we're past the point of needing protection."

"Good point." Grant slanted his mouth over hers while hooking his left arm under her right leg. The next thing she knew, the bed was underneath her and Grant was above her, sliding the tip of his shaft against her damp heat.

"Please," Rebekah begged, sliding her hands down his muscular back and pulling him toward her.

Grant threw back his head and let out a deep moan when he buried himself inside of her. He was raised on his elbows, his chest grazing hers as he searched her eyes. "Sweetheart, I'm trying to hold myself back but if you keep rocking your hips like that, I won't be able to."

Again, she felt that thrilling sensation that her body had this much control over his. She locked her legs behind him and said, "The last thing I want to do right now is hold back."

Chapter Ten

Grant had planned to take things slowly, to savor each moment, but Rebekah was so eager and so encouraging. When she started making those little hiccuping sounds in his ear and then shuddered in his arms, he lost all control.

She gave another small shudder when he eased onto his side and he kept his hand curled around her waist as he asked, "Are you okay?"

Her eyes remained closed, with her silky lashes fanning her cheeks, but she was able to manage a slight nod and a very satisfied smile.

The past few weeks, he'd rarely seen Rebekah do much more than offer a pleasant grin—and that had usually been directed at someone else. Pride swirled around him at the realization that he'd been the one responsible for this particular smile. He pulled her closer against him, absorbing every inch of her satisfaction through her relaxed muscles.

The sound of tinkling metal filtered in from outside the bedroom, followed by the echo of little claws on the hardwood floors. Rebekah jerked up into a sitting position, taking the top sheet with her and covering that beautiful view. "What's that noise?"

"That's right. You aren't familiar with the pitter-patter of little doggy feet yet." Grant smiled at her embarrassed expression when Angus appeared in the doorway. "Look who's up from his nap."

"He probably needs to go outside for a walk." Rebekah's eyes searched frantically around the room until they landed on the crumpled dress that had landed in a heap a few yards from the bed. "Can you distract him for a second so that he doesn't see me getting dressed?"

Grant smothered a chuckle. "Are you afraid he'll know what we were doing?"

"Don't wiggle your eyebrows at me. This dog is a lot smarter than he looks and he understands way more than he lets on."

"Come on, boy," Grant said, rising to his feet. "Mommy doesn't want you to see her naked and know that we were doing very sexy grown-up things in her bed."

She made a squeaking sound and pointed at Grant. "Now he's seeing you naked."

"Rebekah, I hate to be the one to break it to you, but Angus isn't exactly dressed, either. I don't think he cares what we wear so long as we feed him and take him on walks."

Grant was easily able to dodge the pillow she sent sailing in his direction.

Not bothering to cover his laughter this time, he found his board shorts on the floor and pulled them on right before the second pillow hit him straight in the forehead.

"Mommy's got a good arm." He scooped up Angus so that the little dog didn't have to keep jumping to see what was going on in the bed eighteen inches above him. The dog gave a happy yip when he saw Rebekah, so Grant placed him right on her lap.

"That's because Mommy went to Duke on a softball scholarship," she told the dog as she scratched him behind the ears. The motion caused the cotton sheet to drop and Rebekah quickly yanked it up over her breasts again. Angus, on the other hand, mistook her quest for modesty as an invitation to play tug-of-war with her bed linens.

"Attaboy, Angus." Grant cheered on the scrappy mutt, who was now growling and yanking for all he was worth. "Get those covers away from her. Don't let her hide that perfect body from me anymore."

Rebekah let the dog win so that she could launch a third pillow in Grant's direction. This time he caught it and enjoyed the view.

"Okay, boy, we won," he said after Angus got himself so tangled up in the sheet, he rolled off the bed and landed in a pile of bedding. Grant picked up the happy dog in one arm and scooped his T-shirt off the ground with the other as he walked toward the bedroom door.

"How about I take you for a walk while Mommy recovers from Daddy's skilled lovemaking?"

A fourth pillow hit the doorjamb as Rebekah yelled out, "Stop talking to him about that!"

Angus took his time as Grant walked him around the property, sniffing every tree, flower and curb along the way. He kept expecting the dog to try and make a run for it, or to at least pull against his leash, but Angus seemed content sticking close to Grant's side.

The poor mutt must still have been groggy from the sedative and the trauma of the day's big adventure because as soon as they returned to the townhome, Angus crashed out again on the sofa. Rebekah had taken a shower while they were gone, and when Grant saw her emerge from the bedroom in a pair of dark blue lounge pants and an oversize Duke softball sweatshirt, he realized that he preferred this casual outfit to the formal clothes she tended to wear all the time.

"I didn't order dinner yet because I wasn't sure what kind of food you liked," she said as she pulled her hair up into a ponytail. It should've sounded weird—the fact that he was having children with a woman and neither of them knew whether the other preferred Italian or Chinese for takeout.

However, the neckline of her sweatshirt dropped to the side and exposed a bare shoulder and suddenly Grant didn't care about food at all.

He leaned over to kiss her gently, and she gazed at him, then took his hand to lead him back to her bedroom—this time closing the door softly behind them to make sure Angus wouldn't distract them.

After another round of lovemaking they agreed on pizza, which was delivered while Grant used Rebekah's shower.

"I guess eating on the sofa is out of the question since Angus has established that as his new bed," Grant said after he emerged from the bathroom. The dog gave him a dismissive glance before burrowing deeper into the throw pillows. "That's a pretty big improvement from the dank porch you slept under last night, huh, big guy?"

"Actually, I was hoping you wouldn't mind me working through dinner. I need to go over a draft for the latest grant proposal I'm putting together for the animal shelter." Rebekah had her back to him and was pulling plates out of a kitchen cabinet. "I was supposed to do it today at the office, but then..."

She trailed off as she stared at the pup relaxing on her furniture. The zesty smell of pepperoni and tomato sauce surrounded them and Grant tugged at the neck of the clean T-shirt he'd found in his carry-on bag. It would've been quite the homey scene if he'd actually felt at home here in her living room. Or even in her presence.

Rebekah was looking everywhere but at him and he suddenly had the feeling that maybe he'd been too presumptuous in bringing his overnight bag upstairs. Sure, he'd spent the night here a couple of months ago, but that had been a one-off. Grant didn't usually play house with the women he dated.

Not that he and Rebekah were actually dating. They were just sleeping together. And having kids together. And pretending to be in a relationship so that everyone else around them would think they were…together.

Hell. Grant scratched at his damp head. He was supposed to be the guy who usually got people out of sticky situations. So how, exactly, had he ended up in this situation with no exit strategy in sight?

He cleared his throat. "That's cool. I actually have a presentation I need to work on. We're setting up a product launch for my company's latest design of waterproof cases for video equipment."

They sat down on opposites sides of the table and hid behind their respective laptops as they ate. Despite the fact that there were so many things that needed to be said between them, so many decisions that needed to be made, neither one of them spoke while they worked.

She would yawn. He would ask if she was tired—according to the pregnancy book he'd just finished, she should be—and she would insist that she was fine and continue clicking away at her keyboard. Yep. She was definitely avoiding something. Grant glanced down the hall to her open bedroom door. So far, the bed was the one place where things weren't awkward between them.

After an hour, Angus roused himself enough to jump to the floor and sniff his way to the front door. Rebekah finally looked up from her screen. "Do you think he needs to go outside again?"

"I'll take him." Grant didn't know about Angus, but he was dying to go out and take a break from this tense silence. He slammed his laptop closed and sprang up to get the dog's leash.

"Thank you," Rebekah said around another yawn. She'd resumed her typing before he and Angus were even out the front door.

"Any suggestions on how I can get her to open up?" Grant asked the dog a few minutes later as they followed their earlier route around the perimeter of the property. In response, Angus lifted his leg against one of the decorative lampposts.

"It's not like she can avoid the topic of…*you know*… forever," Grant continued, more to himself than to the canine who kept on walking. "The woman can't even say the word *pregnancy*. She just calls it *you know* all the time. So how am I supposed to figure out what she wants when she won't tell me?"

Angus tilted his head and gave him a lopsided look. "You're right, I shouldn't be out here talking to a dog about this. I need to go back in there and have a conversation with her."

As they made their way back to her door, Grant made a mental outline of everything he wanted to say to Rebekah. Unfortunately, when he got inside, he found her with her head slumped onto the table near the keyboard of her laptop. Sound asleep.

Rebekah sneaked a peek at Grant's sleeping form next to her and then squeezed her eyes shut as she buried her face deeper in the pillow. She had a hazy recollection of him carrying her from the table to her room last night, and she supposed that after everything else they'd done in this bed together, it was probably only natural for him to assume that they should sleep there together, as well.

However, waking up next to the man felt as though she was going in the opposite direction of where she needed to be. She was supposed to be getting him out of her life. Or, at least, not building up her expectations for having him in it on a permanent basis.

Her hands fisted in frustration at how easy it had been to fall under his spell again. When her ex-boyfriend had found out she was pregnant a few years ago, it had led to a swift breakup. Sure, it had been heartbreaking at the time, but at least Trey hadn't lingered, making promises that he knew he never truly intended to keep.

Logically, Rebekah knew she shouldn't be comparing the two men, especially while one of them was still in her bed. And really, Trey and Grant were as different as night and day. Her ex had been focused, steady; she'd always known what to expect with him, even down to his unbending intentions to never be a father. But Grant was so…was so…she lifted her arms to cover her head in frustration. She didn't even know what Grant was, or more important, what to expect from him.

All she knew was that, against her better judgment, she was attracted to him and she could easily be swayed into believing his promises if she let her guard down around him. She also knew that she wasn't about to waste another six years of her life on a man who wouldn't stay by her side no matter what.

She attempted to scoot her body toward the side of

the bed, but Grant immediately rolled with her, stretching an arm across her waist. As the sheets shifted, a growl sounded from between their two bodies.

Grant's eyes were closed as he tousled the dog's ears. "Is Mommy stealing your sheets again, Angus?"

"What happened to his spot on the sofa?" Rebekah sat up gently. She'd recently learned that moving too quickly in the morning could bring on an extra bout of queasiness.

"He came in here in the middle of night and was whimpering on your side of the bed. I didn't want him to wake you, so I just pulled him up here with us."

With us. Rebekah had always slept alone, and suddenly she was sharing her bed with both a man and a dog. How had things gone from pretend dating to this?

Her phone vibrated on the bedside table. She'd had it beside her when she was working last night, so Grant must've carried it in here, too. She saw the name on the screen and gasped. "It's your Aunt Bunny."

"Tell her I said good-morning." Grant stretched, the bare muscles of his shoulders and chest on prominent display. Her eyes immediately went downward, her mind straying toward thoughts of what was under the sheet. Apparently, he was perfectly comfortable making himself at home in her bed.

"I'm not answering it." Rebekah sent the call to voice mail. "And I'm definitely not telling her you said hello or anything else that might make her think that you're here with me."

"I'm sure Birdie told her yesterday that I was staying the night to help keep an eye on Angus. Plus, your car is still in the parking lot at Furever Paws. She's probably calling to give you last-minute instructions about our visit to the bird sanctuary."

"Oh, no, I forgot about the bird sanctuary." She looked at Grant. "Do we really have to go there today?"

"Have you met Aunt Bunny? I know she's the more forgetful aunt, but when it comes to animals, she can be pretty focused and determined."

Rebekah's phone immediately rang again and Grant said, "Which means she's not going to stop calling you until she knows we're on the road."

He gave her a wink, then stood up and practically strutted to the bathroom.

Yep. He'd been totally, comfortably nude under that sheet.

Why hadn't Rebekah insisted on setting some boundaries between them last night? She asked herself that question for the eight hundredth time as they drove down Route 64 along the Albemarle Sound.

Instead, she'd had sex with him—twice—then pretended to work during dinner before falling asleep and waking up with Grant in her bed. Never in her life had Rebekah been so reluctant to face a challenge or make hard decisions. She squeezed her eyes shut behind her dark sunglasses.

This whole pregnancy must be doing something strange to her emotions. That was the only explanation that made any sense.

Hell, she'd even agreed to foster a dog yesterday.

She glanced behind her at Angus, who'd taken over the

back seat of Grant's rental car the same way he'd taken over her sofa. Grant wasn't doing anything to rein him in…but to be fair, neither was she—and that was totally unlike her. Clearly, she wasn't making logical decisions.

Which was why she'd been even more determined to go to this bird sanctuary at her boss's request to gather as much information as she could for a full report and recommendation. If Rebekah kept her mind focused on work, she wouldn't have to worry about her thoughts slipping to how perfectly she'd fit in Grant's arms last night. Or how perfectly formed his body had looked this morning as he'd walked around her townhome half-dressed.

Despite the fact that her morning sickness was now flirting with possible car sickness, she mostly kept her eyes glued to the tablet on her lap as she researched the bird sanctuary and made notes about their business model.

"Go ahead and email me the notes from those focus group discussions." Grant spoke into his wireless Bluetooth, the one he'd been using for the entire two hours that they'd been on the road. "I'll take a look at them before the video conference call with the retail suppliers this afternoon."

Rebekah didn't feel so bad about avoiding conversation with the guy when he clearly had his own business matters to handle. Of course, it also made her question why a busy man like Grant was spending so much time in North Carolina lately—helping out his aunts with things that Rebekah or other members of the Furever Paws staff could probably be doing.

Before she could ask as much, Angus's ears perked up as the car slowed to take the highway exit and he lifted his paws onto one windowsill before marching along the back seat to observe the scenery out of the other window.

Grant lifted his eyes to the rearview mirror. "Laird Angus looks like he's standing sentry along the castle keep, going from one watchtower to the next."

Just like her, the animal seemed much more apprehensive than excited about arriving at their destination.

"Maybe I should've left him at home," Rebekah said. What she really meant was perhaps both she *and* the dog should've stayed home.

"Remember, Birdie thought it'd be a good idea to get Angus out and try to socialize him a bit more. See how he interacts with other people and animals."

It turned out that Angus did fine interacting with the office staff. In fact, he was so quiet and so low to the ground, Rebekah had to wonder if anyone behind the counters had even seen him. It was the socializing with other animals that soon became a problem. Angus went nuts at the sight of the flamingos near the entrance and barked his little furry head off, straining at his leash in his attempts to try and round up the birds as though they were a flock of sheep.

"We usually only allow service animals," the director explained as Grant laughed at Angus's antics while Rebekah tried to shush the dog and get him under control.

Rebekah had a sudden glimpse into what raising children with Grant would be like. He'd be the playful one, the parent who would indulge their children in sugar and wrestling matches and get them all amped up before bedtime. And Rebekah would be the rule enforcer, the parent who made them eat their vegetables and wash their hands.

Her gaze narrowed and Grant must've picked up on her annoyance because he cleared his throat and said, "Why don't I take Angus out front to the park and let him run around while you take the tour?"

To the park? To have fun while Rebekah did all the work? Not that taking a tour was necessarily work but taking thorough notes so she could report back to Bunny and Birdie afterward would require quite an effort. Especially when Rebekah already knew that she'd have to inform them that there was no way Furever Paws could accommodate birds with their limited budget. There was no way to save all the animals all the time.

"Actually," Rebekah responded. "Since this was *your* trip initially, why don't *you* go on the tour and *I'll* take Angus out and play?"

She didn't wait for a response, but scooped the still-barking dog into her arms and carried him toward the exit. Maybe it was childish and petty, but the sooner she set a precedent of Grant taking on his fair share of the menial, less playful tasks, the sooner she could prove that he wasn't cut out for long-term fatherhood.

Not that she didn't think her kids needed a father in their lives, but if she kept her expectations of Grant lower, then she wouldn't be setting herself—or their children—up for disappointment when Grant took off at the first sign of trouble.

It hadn't even been a full hour when he came to

find Rebekah and Angus in the park, proving her right. Smugness coursed through her, but there was also a tinge of disappointment. "I see you couldn't last the full two hours for the entire tour."

"No need to." Grant smiled and held up two bottles of water he must've bought in the gift shop. "I'd already researched the place last week when Bunny mentioned it to me, and the director had answered most of my questions in an email a few days ago. If my aunt was here, she'd want to see each and every bird, but I'm more of a dog guy myself, right Angus?"

Grant handed Rebekah one of the bottles and then knelt down next to the dog and poured some water into a cupped hand. Angus eagerly lapped it up and Rebekah sizzled with guilt for not thinking about the fact that the dog might be thirsty. It had to be eighty degrees in the shade, and she was gulping her water just as greedily as he was.

She wiped her mouth on the back of her wrist, trying to make the action as ladylike as possible. "So if you'd already done the research, and you didn't plan to see the birds, why'd we drive all the way here?"

He could've at least mentioned something before she'd made herself carsick staring at her tablet for over two hours of the ride, learning everything she possibly could about the bird sanctuary.

"Because my aunt asked me to." He rose to his feet as if that explained a perfectly logical waste of Rebekah's entire day. "The director told me there's a great restaurant a couple of miles down the sound. It has outdoor seating and is dog friendly. You wanna grab some lunch, boy?"

Angus yipped and tugged on his leash as he led the humans toward the car.

"Or we could head back to Spring Forest and I could get some actual work done today," Rebekah suggested.

"You know," Grant said as he opened her passenger door, "it's okay to take the day off every once in a while."

Rebekah felt her eyes narrow and it took every ounce of control not to unleash her annoyance at him. She still wasn't exactly sure what Grant did at his job—besides make things sound better than they were. But he apparently did it well.

Maybe she could use their lunch detour as an opportunity to find out something more about the guy who'd fathered her children. At this point, the only things she knew with any degree of certainty were that he was infuriating…and good in bed.

Chapter Eleven

Good thing Grant wasn't trying to impress anyone at lunch with their pretend relationship because this fish-and-chips stand was far from romantic. But at least it was outdoors and airy, which hopefully meant the smell of seafood was less likely to make Rebekah queasy. The place was packed, and they ended up having to share one of the wooden patio tables with a family of five. The crab cakes were amazing, though, and the tartar sauce was the best he'd ever tasted.

He couldn't really have anything resembling a private conversation with Rebekah because they were stuck next to a toddler who kept stealing French fries off of her mom's plate and giving them to Angus under the table. The five-year-old boy wanted to know who Grant's third favorite superhero was, the preteen was watching music videos on her phone at full blast, and the parents kept apologizing to Grant and Rebekah for the chaos.

An older couple with an overweight dachshund sat down at the table next to them and suddenly Angus had some competition for the French fries that were now being stolen off Rebekah's plate, as well.

Because the dog had been living on the streets for so long, Grant wasn't sure how well Angus would do sharing food with the plump, sausage-shaped dog.

"Come on, boy." Grant took the leash from where Rebekah had looped it up to her elbow. Then he picked up his used plate and the used napkins closest to him and told the dog, "Let's go down to the beach and take a little walk before we get back in the car."

Rebekah caught up to him near the trash cans. "Why do you always do that?"

"Do what?"

"Take off for the fun walks and leave me with the work."

"What work?" he wanted to know.

"Well, earlier, it was the tour at the bird sanctuary. And just now it was…" She paused as she looked down at the plastic tray with the remainder of their trash. He took it out of her hands and disposed of it just before a seagull landed on the trash can and squawked at them.

"Listen, I would've taken your plate for you, but Angus was already straining on the leash and you didn't look as though you were quite done with your food."

"I was done as soon as the little girl started swiping my fries with fingers covered in dog saliva." Rebekah pulled a bottle of antibacterial gel out of her enormous tote bag and squirted a stream onto her hands. "Where are you going?"

"I was going to take Angus down to the beach for a walk. Remember?"

"I thought you were just saying that as an excuse to get away from all the kids and that mean wiener dog who kept growling at him."

"Well, it was partly an excuse, but I also thought it would be fun to let him play near the water."

"Are you sure dogs are allowed down here?" she asked as they walked along the wooden planks toward the sand below. There weren't many people out here since it was a weekday afternoon.

"I didn't see a sign forbidding it." Grant bent over to unhook Angus's leash.

"What are you doing?" Rebekah placed a hand on his shoulder. "What if he runs away?"

"Let's give him a little freedom and see what he does," Grant suggested. Noting her response, he then added, "What was that for?"

"What?" she asked.

"You just rolled your eyes at me. And now you're doing that huffy breath thing. If you're mad about something, you can just tell me."

"Let's just say I'm starting to get a glimpse of how it's going to be if we decide to coparent. You'll always be the fun one, giving the kids all kinds of freedom and letting them get away with everything. And I'm going to be the rule enforcer that they never want to be with."

"What do you mean, *if* we decide to coparent?" Something twisted in his gut and he didn't think it was just the fried food from lunch. "I told you already that I plan to be in our children's lives. So it's not a matter of *if* we coparent but *how* we coparent that we need to discuss."

Rebekah's eyes were clear and calculating as she studied him. But she didn't offer a rebuttal. Or anything else that would constitute an actual discussion of the very topic she'd been avoiding for the past couple of weeks. Grant put his hands on his hips, ready to get the battle of words out of the way once and for all.

Rebekah sighed. "Fine, you can let him off the leash. But if he takes off, I'm not going to be able to chase after him in these heels."

It wasn't the concession he wanted to hear from her, but he had the sense that it was the best he'd be getting right now. Grant shrugged. "Then take your shoes off and experience the relaxing feeling of being the fun parent. Let me worry about Angus."

She swallowed a groan, then braced herself against him as she removed her strappy sandals. He flexed his biceps under her hand as she balanced herself on one foot and then the other.

"Now your turn, boy," he told the dog as he bent again to unhook the leash. Luckily, Angus didn't run away. But he did run to the edge of the water and then back again. In fact, he did several laps, and when Grant found a piece of driftwood, he gave it a little toss to see what the dog would do.

Angus proudly retrieved the driftwood and carried it back, dropping it at Rebekah's feet. She laughed and threw it again for him, and Grant decided he could stand here all day, watching her laughing and playing with the dog. Eventually, the stick ended up in the water and Angus barked at it, as though he could order the wood to return to the shore.

Grant slipped out of his flip-flops and walked into the water. When he was up to his knees Angus let out a series of happy yips and came crashing into the water near him.

"No!" Rebekah yelled. "Grab him before he drowns."

But the dog's short legs began paddling and Angus deftly motored his little body to the stick and retrieved it before easily making his way back to the sand.

"Look who's a natural at swimming," Grant said excitedly. He threw the stick back in the water over and over again, and Angus eagerly retrieved it every time.

"I think I'm going to need to take you out on the waves with me one day," he told the dog, who was now panting lazily at Rebekah's feet.

"No way," Rebekah said. "He's too little to go surfing."

Angus's response was to shake water all over her.

Grant knew that Rebekah cared way more about the dog than she was letting on. In fact, he had a feeling that she cared far too much about a lot of things, and that's why she wasn't allowing Grant to get too close to her. To test his theory, he bent down to clip the leash to Angus's collar and said, "Is that your way of telling Mommy that you want to go surfing with Daddy? Maybe we'll teach your brothers or sisters how to surf, too."

Rebekah didn't roll her eyes this time. Instead she looked at the clock on her phone screen. "We should probably get going before we end up stuck in rush-hour traffic."

Apparently, playtime was over.

* * *

Grant figured the rental car company would be adding a cleaning charge to his bill to get rid of the wet, salty dog smell from the back seat. But seeing Angus enjoy the water so much made the extra expense well worth it.

"So what are you going to tell your aunts about the bird sanctuary?" Rebekah asked when they finally pulled out of the parking lot. It was nice to have her full attention, where her head wasn't buried behind a laptop or an electronic tablet.

"I'm going to tell them that it's a great program, but the licensing requirements they operate under are way too narrow to be a fit for what they want to accomplish. Furever Paws has too many species for something like this to make sense on my aunts' property. With their finances being so strained, it just isn't feasible in the foreseeable future."

"I agree. You know, I see how close you are to your aunts, and it makes me wonder why you haven't spoken to your Uncle Gator on their behalf."

The skin along the back of Grant's neck prickled. "Spoken to my uncle about what, exactly?"

"Oh, you know. You could use your smooth-talking marketing skills and put in a strong word to him and suggest that he repay that missing money."

Grant was glad that the light to the highway on-ramp had turned red and he didn't have to pull over to the side of the road so he could pivot and face Rebekah. "You actually think my uncle has something to do with their investments going bad?"

"It doesn't appear to be as simple as just some failed investments."

"Are you saying they suspect it was embezzlement? That my aunts believe this, too?" A heavy weight settled in the pit of Grant's stomach and he wanted to have this out, convince her she was wrong, but a horn sounded behind them and he had to resume driving.

"I'm not sure what exactly your aunts believe at this point. But I think it's a little odd that you are always in town to help boost their revenue, but you've never really questioned why there was a need to boost it in the first place."

"It's not odd," Grant said.

"Is burying your head in the sand a better way to put it?"

"Is that what you think I'm doing, Rebekah?" It was on the tip of Grant's tongue to suggest that she should be familiar enough with the concept, seeing as how they walked on eggshells every time the subject of her pregnancy came up. But he decided to come at it from a different angle. "I prefer to believe that people are innocent until proven guilty."

They both knew that Rebekah kept expecting the worst where he was concerned, but he couldn't tell if his words had hit their mark because Rebekah didn't take the bait. She simply held herself stiffly, her eyes fixed on a spot outside the windshield.

The outside sounds of traffic filtered in and the urge to say something else pressed against the back of his throat. Eventually she would come to see that Grant was serious about being a father. Eventually, he'd prove himself to her. But it wasn't going to happen today. And in the meantime, his uncle wasn't there to speak for himself and needed defending more.

After at least ten minutes had gone by, he finally spoke. "Listen, there's no way Uncle Gator would do that to his own sisters. At least, not intentionally. I mean, he can be a little arrogant, but that's because he really is good at what he does. It's how he made his fortune. That doesn't make him a crook—especially not when it comes to his family. Whitakers look out for each other. You don't know him, so you don't trust him. Fine, that's understandable. But even if you don't believe me when I say that that's something he just wouldn't do, there's also the fact that it doesn't make sense. It's just not logical. With all the money he has, he doesn't need to steal from Bunny and Birdie."

"It wasn't my place to bring it up." She shifted her legs to the side, so that her body was angled toward the door, as though she were dismissing him. "Forget I said anything."

Emotionally, he wanted to say that she was right and it really wasn't her place to discuss his family's issues. However, logically, he knew that she oversaw the finances for the animal shelter and was merely repeating what she'd heard from the people who'd been hired to look directly into the matter.

Still.

"Obviously, there was some mismanagement of finances going on, and obviously it happened under Gator's watch. But that doesn't mean it was intentional." At this point, Grant didn't know if he was trying to convince her or himself. There was no way his uncle was capable of something so underhanded. The whole thing had to be an accident or a misunderstanding. "It's just that you don't know Uncle Gator like we do."

"You're right. I probably don't really know any of you Whitakers. I just work for your family."

Grant felt frustration vibrating against the back of his throat, but he held the groan back, not wanting to insult her any further. "I'm not saying you don't know any of us. You're around Aunt Bunny and Aunt Birdie every day and they're pretty much an open book. Obviously, you know me better than anyone else who works there..."

He trailed off when she tilted her head his way and cocked an eyebrow at him. Okay, so she was probably right to question that statement. They knew each other physically, but did either of them really know the other that well? That was a whole other conversation, though.

"My point is that my family dynamics—especially where Uncle Gator is concerned—are kind of complex."

She leaned her elbow against the door so she could prop her head on her hand. "If you say so."

"Hear me out," Grant said, even as he was thinking she probably would've preferred to take a nap. "My dad was the first of the Whitaker siblings to sell their property. He made a modest amount, but when he moved to Florida, he funneled all that money into the surf shop originally owned by my mom's parents. Gator always gave my dad a hard time about choosing his wife's family over the Whitakers. Anytime I came to visit over the summer, my uncle would immediately welcome me into the fold and would often remind me that family should always take care of each other."

"So that explains why you're often in town helping out your aunts," Rebekah said.

"It also explains why Gator couldn't have possibly embezzled that money. At least, not intentionally. He has always been adamant about looking out for his sisters."

"You said not intentionally," Rebekah pointed out. "So isn't it possible that Gator took the money thinking that he could eventually pay it back? Which is still, by definition, embezzlement."

"I know the definition of embezzlement." Grant gripped the steering wheel defensively. "You're not the only one who took business courses in college."

"I guess your constant beach attire threw me off," she replied, confirming his suspicion that she never took him seriously. She yawned. "Look, I don't want to argue with you about your uncle or your family's finances."

"Then what do you want to argue with me about?" he asked. "Because you sure as hell don't seem to want to talk to me about our children."

He'd made that layered comment earlier about being innocent until proven guilty and it had taken every fiber of strength she possessed not to remind him that, with two children on the way, her first duty was to protect them. If that meant holding reserving judgment until Grant proved himself, then so be it.

Rebekah knew she should now take the opening, to explain to him all of her fears about becoming a mother. But she also just wanted to close her eyes and nap. Unfortunately, her phone rang and she wasn't able to do either.

She looked down at the screen resting in the center console cupholder. "It's my mom."

"I figured that, based on the word MOM across the top and the big picture of Sheila Taylor underneath." Grant's voice held a sarcastic edge and she couldn't really blame him for being frustrated at the interruption.

"I'll let it go to voice mail," Rebekah offered.

"No, go ahead and take it. Our conversation has waited this long. It can certainly wait another few minutes."

Rebekah slid her finger across the screen. "Hi, Mom."

"Hey, Dimples. Your dad and I are running late. We won't get to the restaurant until after six."

"What restaurant?" Rebekah glanced at Grant as though he could tell her that she wasn't crazy.

"Aren't we supposed to meet you and Grant for dinner tonight?" her mom asked. "I have it in the calendar app you set up for me."

"That was last Tuesday, Mom. Did you set it up as a repeat event again?"

Her mom said something, but her voice was muffled, probably because she'd pulled the phone away from her ear and was tapping at her screen. Finally, she came back on. "Yep. It looks like we're having dinner with you two every Tuesday and Friday for the next five years."

Rebekah's phone pinged with a message. She glanced down, then sighed. "Dad's texting me. He wants me to know that you guys will be running late tonight. So I guess his calendar got scheduled wrong, too."

Grant gave her a side-eye and she lowered her phone and said, "My parents are wonderful with kids, not so great with technology. They thought we were supposed to have dinner tonight."

"Who are you talking to?" her mom asked, and Rebekah realized she should've covered the receiver.

"I'm in the car with Grant. We had to go to a bird sanctuary near the Outer Banks. We're on our way home now."

"Oh, that's perfect, then. If you're on Highway 64, we can just meet you in Raleigh and nobody will be late."

"But, Mom, we didn't actually have dinner scheduled." Rebekah squeezed her eyes shut.

"We can stop and meet them for dinner," Grant offered a little too loudly.

"Actually, we can't." Rebekah saw a spot of gray fur on the back seat and her heart lunged with hope. "We have Angus with us."

Upon hearing his name, the dog lifted his head and let out a half-hearted yip.

"Who's Angus?" Sheila asked. "Is that a dog?"

"He's one of the dogs from the shelter. I'm fostering him. Temporarily."

"Since when did you become a dog person, Dimples?"

"Long story," Rebekah grumbled.

"Good thing we'll have time for you to tell us over dinner."

"But, Mom, I just said we can't meet for dinner because we have a dog with us."

"I'm sure we could find a pet-friendly restaurant in Raleigh," Grant offered a little too cheerfully, considering the fact that he'd just gotten done telling her to stay out of *his* family's business. So why wasn't he staying out of hers?

Rebekah could feel her eyes widening in horror as she shook her head at him while simultaneously putting a finger to her lips. But she was too late.

"I'll start looking for a place now," Sheila said happily. "I'll call you back."

Over the next hour, her mom called three more times with questions about what time they would arrive—five o'clock; Grant's favorite type of food—Mexican; and Grant's second-favorite type of food since Via Rancheros only allowed service animals. In between those calls were her dad's texts with screenshots of his calendar app settings and follow-up questions about how to reset the year.

Really, it wasn't Rebekah's fault that she and Grant never got the opportunity to talk about her pregnancy again before they arrived at the restaurant. If Grant had kept quiet when her mom called, they wouldn't be going to dinner with her parents in the first place.

Ever since she'd first slept with the man, nothing had gone as planned. It was as though they were reading the same instructional manual, but they were always on different steps in the assembly process.

If they couldn't get on the same page and have an actual conversation, then how would they ever manage to truly parent their babies together?

Chapter Twelve

When they arrived at the restaurant, Rebekah went straight to the restroom. She'd gone before they left the beach, but her bladder seemed to be holding less, while her stomach was trying to hold more.

Although, currently she had no appetite whatsoever. She wanted to blame it on the fact that they'd had a late lunch, but really it was because her tummy was a bundle of nerves. Grant had met her parents before, but this would be the first time they had the chance to ask him all those questions Rebekah hadn't been able to answer herself last Tuesday.

You can do this, she told herself in the mirror over the sink. But the reflection staring back at her didn't look too convinced. Taking a deep breath, she steeled her spine and headed back to the restaurant lobby. She only hesitated when she saw that her parents had already spotted Grant and Angus.

"Nice to see you again, Mrs. Taylor." He held out his hand in greeting, but her mom pulled him into a tight hug instead.

Angus, of course, loved her dad. It was like an animal instinctively knew when a person was trying to avoid it because they then centered all their attention on that one individual.

"I hope you took your allergy medicine, Mike," her mom said as the dog sniffed away at her father's freckled legs below his cargo shorts.

"I did, but I'll sit on the other side of the table, just in case." Her father gave her a quick peck on the forehead. "Looking healthy, Dimples."

Her dad must have been lying because two minutes ago in the bathroom mirror she'd looked anything but healthy. At least, mentally. But she appreciated the sentiment all the same.

"So tell me how you ended up a dog mom," her mother said when everyone finally took their seats on the patio.

The server brought a small dog dish with water and took their drink orders while Rebekah told them the story about Angus, leaving out the parts where she'd sat on the porch of an abandoned house talking to the stray dog. "There wasn't any room at the shelter to house him last night, so we took him home."

"We?" Her dad wiggled his eyebrows before giving her mom a knowing look. Oh, great. She hadn't meant to let that part slip. But it did kind of add to this whole pretense that she and Grant were actually together.

"Here, boy, don't lick that," Grant said to Angus, who was going to town on a spot of spilled barbecue sauce under the table. At least, Rebekah hoped it was just sauce.

"Sounds like you and Grant are getting a test run at being parents." Her mother smiled. "How's it going?"

Rebekah opened her mouth to argue that it wasn't like that, but Grant spoke up first. "So far, so good. I have a feeling that twins are going to be a little bit more work—although this guy eats enough for two."

Her parents laughed and Rebekah felt her molars grinding at the fact that Grant could so easily make jokes about their situation. That he could be so casual and unaffected about the amount of stress that they'd be under less than a year from now. But that was Grant, always making things sound better than they were. The guy currently had his charm level turned up to the lay-it-on-thick setting.

"It's actually taken some adjusting," Rebekah said. "I was away from my office today and now I'm behind on everything."

"You'll get to it, sweetheart," Grant said, placing his hand along the back of her neck. Rebekah practically shot out of her chair before she remembered that they were supposed to be pretending to be in a loving relationship. "Those budget reports will still be there when you get back on Monday."

He used his thumb to massage the knot forming between her shoulder blades and it felt so amazing, she wanted to arch her neck and moan in delight. But they were sitting across from her parents and his words only brought on more anxiety. "Yeah, they'll still be there when I get back, along with all the work I'm supposed to do on Monday, as well."

Her mom leaned forward to grab a piece of cornbread from the basket, then offered the mini crock of honey butter to Grant. "Our daughter has always been very orderly. Never liked leaving anything to the last minute. But you've probably already picked up on that."

"I got that impression the first time I met her." Grant nodded before taking a big gulp of his sweet tea. "And then it was reaffirmed when I saw that her townhome was set up like one of those model homes. Not so much as a dish in the sink or a throw pillow out of place."

"Sorry to break it to you, Dimples," her father chuckled. "But as soon as those babies start walking, you can kiss that fancy white sofa and all those breakable knick-knacks goodbye."

Rebekah gulped. She loved that sofa. It had been her first major purchase after college and it made her feel like an adult who was in complete control of her life. The thought of changing her whole living room just to accommodate children had her tapping her feet under the table.

"You should've seen her watching Angus last night when he got up on that couch." Grant teased. "She kept glancing over at his paws for any sign of dirt."

"That sounds like Rebekah, all right," her mother agreed. "No time for messes in her schedule."

The server came to take their order and Grant kept

his hand casually draped along her shoulders as he whispered to her. "I'm not very hungry. Do you want to share something?"

In an effort to seem less controlling than everyone at the table was making her appear, she gave a stiff nod and said, "Sure. I'll just have a couple of bites of whatever you get."

"We'll take the sampler platter and the rib combo plate." Grant handed the menu to the server.

"I'd rather have the chicken," she said, then snapped her mouth closed because she'd just proved them all right. "But the ribs are good."

"Apparently, we'll take the chicken and rib platter instead," Grant said to the waiter.

"And what would you like for your three sides?" the man asked.

"How about the barbecue beans," Grant started but Rebekah couldn't keep from scrunching her nose. "Make that the macaroni and cheese." He looked at her. "Do you like coleslaw?"

"I'd rather have the wedge salad. And their onion rings are really great. Maybe some more French fries since Angus ate all of mine earlier?"

"Are you sure you don't want to get two meals, after all?" the server asked.

Rebekah realized she hadn't been sure of anything for a long time.

Grant knew that Rebekah was anxious as hell, because he could feel her leg nervously fidgeting beside his all through the meal. But he was actually enjoying his dinner with Mike and Sheila Taylor. They were full of stories about their daughter and they asked all the hard questions that Rebekah had been avoiding until now.

"So do you plan to stay home from work for a while after the twins get here? Or are you looking into childcare and nannies?" Mike Taylor asked as he slipped a piece of brisket to Angus under the table.

The dog's manners were going to be atrocious after all the dining excursions today, but Grant wasn't about to say anything that would distract Rebekah from her father's question.

"We haven't decided that yet," she said before polishing off a piece of cornbread. If Grant had a dollar for every time she'd given that same response, he could pay the nanny's first week's salary. If they decided to go with a nanny.

"Grant, are you okay with Rebekah going back to work full-time?" Sheila asked and Grant gave Rebekah a sideways glance.

"Obviously, I'm okay with whatever makes Rebekah happy."

"Good. That was a trick question." Sheila nodded at him before turning to her daughter. "Although, if you can take some time off to bond with the twins at first, that would be ideal."

"Mom, you know I'm not very good with babies," Rebekah admitted. Grant leaned back in his chair to carefully listen to this new revelation that explained at least some of why Rebekah had been so uneasy discussing the pregnancy.

"That's crazy," her dad said. "Anybody can handle a baby."

"Really?" Rebekah drew back her chin in disbelief. "You know all those babies you guys fostered? Did I ever interact with any of them?"

Her mom folded her hands together, giving Grant the impression that the woman was ready to get down to business. "You did with Janelle."

"Who?" Rebekah asked, a frown line forming above her nose.

"You might not remember her because you were so young when she left," Mike said, then exchanged a glance with Sheila, who gave him a nod of encouragement. "Dimples, when you were two years old, you started asking for a little brother or sister. That's all you wanted for Christmas, for your birthday, for Valentine's Day. Your mom and I tried to conceive, but no luck. I mean, we really, really tried. Every morning and night we were at it. Babe, remember that lovemaking schedule—"

Rebekah covered her ears. "Gross, Dad. Nobody wants to hear about you guys and your schedule."

"Anyway, when we realized that we couldn't conceive, we started seriously talking about all the other options. We researched adoption and filled out questionnaires and talked to attorneys and social workers and decided fostering was the way to go. Janelle was the first baby we brought home from the hospital. You were four years old and you loved her like crazy. You thought she was your own baby. We had her for six months and then got the call that the court was going to start the reunification process with her biological family. When she left, you were absolutely inconsolable."

Sheila reached across the table to pat Rebekah's hand. "Initially, we were planning to give you time to get over Janelle's leaving, but the agency called us the next week and needed an emergency foster for just a few days. When we brought *that* baby home, you wanted absolutely nothing to do with it. In fact, after Janelle left, you stopped playing with your dolls and even your stuffed animals altogether."

"I don't remember any of this," Rebekah said, her forehead creased in confusion. Grant's hand returned to the back of her neck and he stroked the tight muscles underneath the skin, finally understanding why Rebekah had been so apprehensive about motherhood.

"You were very young," Sheila reminded her. "But ever since then, you've always stayed away from babies and smaller kids. You even stayed away from animals, which was why we were so happy to find out that you'd taken the job at Furever Paws. We were hoping you were coming around."

Mike clapped his palms together. "And now here you are, pregnant and fostering a dog of your own. When it rains, it pours."

Rebekah sat at the table, numbly nodding her head at her parents as Grant paid the check and then made plans to see them again in a couple of weeks. She was sure there'd been some talk of double strollers and ultrasound appointments, but she'd been lost in her own memories, Grant's reassuring hand along her spine the only thing that kept her grounded in the present.

"Are you feeling okay?" Grant asked as he climbed into the driver's seat ten minutes later. When he'd opened the passenger door for Rebekah, Angus had decided to jump up onto her lap instead of claiming the back seat. "It's like the dog senses something's wrong and he's trying to console you."

"He probably has a bellyache from all that brisket my dad was feeding him under the table," Rebekah reasoned, even though Angus's black eyes were studying her intently, as though he was looking for some sort of sign that everything would be okay. She stroked the dog's back. "Let's get you home, boy."

"Rebekah, I'm not starting the car until you tell me what's bugging you. You mentally checked out toward the end of dinner and I can't make it better if I don't know what's wrong."

"Who says you need to make me feel better? I don't need fixing."

"I'm a fixer. A saver. It's what I do. Now, I've learned to tell when you're mad, when you're annoyed and when you're legitimately busy with work." Grant's chest expanded with his deep breath. "As opposed to when you're just faking being busy with work to get out of talking to me."

She opened her mouth to protest, but he held up his palm. "Hold on. I've also learned when you're flustered, and I've learned when you're overwhelmed and scared about something. Right now, you're clearly scared. So let me help."

"It's not something you can help with. You heard my parents. I'm not a baby person. Yet, here I am, having two of them."

"I believe *you* were the one who claimed you aren't a baby person and your *father* said that was crazy."

"But then they told that story about how I wanted nothing to do with the other babies. What if the twins get here and I feel the same way?"

"Rebekah." Grant lifted her chin, forcing her eyes to meet his. "You were a child when that happened. It was a defense mechanism because you'd already lost someone close to you and didn't want to go through that heartache again. But our kids aren't going anywhere."

"What if something happens to them, though?" She could feel the wetness at the corners of her eyes and tried to blink back the tears.

"Is this about the pregnancy you lost?" He traced his hand along her jaw and up to her ear so he could gently smooth the curls away from her face.

"Yes. I mean, no." She couldn't decide. "Maybe. When I got pregnant back then, it couldn't have come at a worse time. I was still in business school and my boyfriend was adamant that he didn't want kids. I'd been on the pill and never missed a day. But then I'd gotten strep throat and the antibiotics made the birth control ineffective. Trey accused me of getting pregnant on purpose, but I told him that I didn't want a baby any more than he did. We had a huge fight and broke up. A few days later, I found out that the pregnancy wasn't viable and, I know this sounds crazy, but all I could think before the laparoscopic procedure was that my baby had heard me say that I didn't want it. And that's why I…why I…" She couldn't hold back any longer.

"Aww, sweetheart. You can't blame yourself. Not for any of it." He used the back of his hand to wipe the tears trailing down her cheeks and leaned his forehead against hers. "Is that why you keep referring to this pregnancy as *you know*? Because you don't want the twins to hear us talking about them?"

"I guess. But also because I really *am* afraid that I won't be the kind of mom they deserve."

He pulled back and met her gaze. "Look at you with Angus. You're going to be a great mom. You just need to get out of your own head."

"I've only had Angus for twenty-four hours. And you've done half the work with him. What happens when it's just me on my own?"

His hands moved to either side of her face, forcing her to look squarely at him. "That's what I keep trying to tell you. It won't be just you on your own. I'm not going anywhere, Rebekah."

He kissed her damp cheeks, stopping one of the tears from going any farther. She almost believed him.

But then his cell phone rang.

Chapter Thirteen

Rebekah knew that if Bunny or Birdie had called Grant to come fix a leak in their roof, he would've been out the door in an instant. So when his mom had called him the previous evening about the leak in the surf shop, it was no surprise that he'd asked if he could drop off her and Angus so that he could get to the airport and catch a flight home that night.

She appreciated his dedication to his family, but didn't they have roofers and plumbers in Jacksonville? Certainly Grant wasn't the only one who could save the day.

"All I'm saying is that anytime things start getting too intense, he always has to fly back to Florida," she told Angus as he whimpered by the front door as though he was waiting for Grant to walk through any minute. "I know. I'd probably run off, too, if my pregnant fake girl-friend was having an emotional breakdown in my car."

Walking into her bedroom, she stubbed her toe on the corner of his carry-on suitcase, which was still open on her rug. She muffled a curse under her breath.

Angus made a low growl as his triangular ears perked up into points.

"You didn't hear that," she told the dog.

She wanted to pitch the whole suitcase and its contents out her front door, but then she'd have to look at the mess when she left tomorrow. Instead, she threw everything inside—trying not to inhale the scent of Grant on his clothing or remember how his bare skin smelled even better—and zipped it closed before shoving it into the hallway closet.

The guy had only spent a total of two nights here in the past few months, but already his absence was noticeable. As she climbed under the covers that evening, her bed suddenly felt way too huge, way too empty. How could she already miss something she'd never really had?

The following morning, she stared longingly at her coffee machine through half-lidded eyes rimmed with dark circles. A chocolate croissant would come in pretty handy right about now, but her car was still parked at Furever Paws. While she didn't normally work on Saturdays, it was often one of the busiest days of the week for the shelter since that's when they usually had families coming in for adoption events.

So she could either call an Uber to go get her car and possibly catch up on some of the work she'd missed yesterday, or she could sit around her townhome thinking about all those tear-filled emotions she'd unloaded on Grant last night.

She pulled up the Uber app on her phone and grabbed Angus's leash off the entry table. "Looks like we're going to work today, big guy."

The dog was all tail wags and panting out the window for the ride to the shelter. But as soon as the driver pulled away, Angus was glued to her leg, cowering behind her. "Don't be scared," she told him. "I know you don't have great memories of this parking lot, but I'm not going to leave you."

He plopped himself on the gravel, and not wanting to drag him behind her, she scooped him up into her arms and carried him into the lobby.

"I thought I saw your car outside this morning," Birdie said as she came from behind the reception desk. "Did Daddy drop you guys off?"

Rebekah stumbled in surprise and it wasn't until Angus was licking at something in Birdie's hand that she realized the older woman had been talking to the dog, not her.

She wanted to correct her boss and explain that Grant wasn't the dog's daddy. She wasn't even the mommy, for that matter. But arguing at this point would only draw more attention. "No. Grant flew back to Florida last night."

"That boy is always on the go. He's a hard one to pin down." Birdie didn't need to tell Rebekah that. The woman made a *tsking* sound then continued, "You look exhausted, dear. Did the road trip to the bird sanctuary tire you out?"

Crap. With Grant taking off like that last night, it again fell to Rebekah to be the bearer of bad news and tell his aunts that their plans for saving birds wouldn't work. "No. I just didn't get much sleep last night."

"Having a new bundle of joy will do that to you," Birdie said and Rebekah tried to suck in her stomach. "Did you keep Mommy up last night?" she asked, and Rebekah realized that the woman was again talking to the dog.

"He sure did." Rebekah didn't add that Angus had been up half the night whimpering at the door and then pacing the house looking for Grant. Sometime around midnight, she'd heard him wrestle something out from under the bed and saw that he'd found one of Grant's T-shirts. He wouldn't go to sleep until she pulled him—and the shirt—onto the bed with her. "Hopefully, he'll nap in my office so that I can get some work done."

"Is that the little gray dog?" Emma Alvarez asked as she walked through the lobby with her fiancé, Daniel Sutton, and their three girls. "He looks so much better."

"Rebekah is fostering him," Birdie explained.

"We had fosters," Penny, the middle girl, said. "But they were kittens."

"Four of them." Pippa, the youngest girl, held up four fingers. "But now they're gone."

Something tugged at Rebekah's heart. "You must miss them very much."

"Kind of. But they have forever homes now." Paris,

the oldest daughter, sounded as though she was reminding her younger sisters of the positive outcome.

Pippa's smile revealed a missing top tooth. "Emma
and Daddy said we could come see the new cat room
and maybe pick out some more foster kittens that need
us."

"Come on, guys," Penny said, pulling on her father's
hand. When the family walked away, Rebekah stood
there staring at them.

"Sweet family, huh?" Birdie said and Rebekah nearly
jumped because she hadn't realized she'd been caught
gawking.

"Very sweet. But I was just thinking that it must
be very difficult for kids to foster—to bring a pet into
their family and then later have to let go of something
they love so much."

"It isn't exactly easy for the adults, either." The older
woman patted her shoulder. "You just take a little piece
of that animal along with you. It's amazing how much
love your heart can accommodate once you decide to
open it up."

Birdie walked away, probably intending to leave Rebekah thinking about that cryptic statement all day. Instead, all her mind could focus on was the older woman's
earlier words about Grant being a hard one to pin down.

"Can I ask you a question, Mom?" Grant dumped
the last bucket of collected rainwater into the indus-
trial sink in the board-shaping room. A crew of workers was on the surf shop's roof above them, pounding
new shingles into place.

His mother leaned against the push broom she'd been using to sweep up the wet plaster from last night's leak. "What's up, kiddo?"

Lana Whitaker was a slight five foot two, and in her denim cutoffs, Costa Rica Surf Tours T-shirt and bleached-blond hair pulled into low pigtails, she didn't look old enough to be calling anyone kiddo.

"What are your thoughts on Uncle Gator?"

"Your dad's brother?" she asked. "He means well, I guess, but he can come off a little condescending at times."

"Do you think he might be the one responsible for Aunt Bunny and Aunt Birdie having financial issues?"

"Oh, no. I'm staying out of that mess. I learned long ago not to get involved in anything that has to do with Whitaker Acres. I love your aunts like they're my own sisters, but when it comes to that property and what everyone did with their shares, I'm keeping my mouth shut."

"Oh, come on, Mom. Can't you just give me a little insight about your early years with dad's side of the family? I'm sure he'd tell me himself if he were still alive."

"My sweet Moose." His mom lowered her eyes and Grant immediately felt remorse wash through him.

"Sorry, I didn't mean to make you feel sad."

"No, you're right. Your dad's heart was the biggest thing about him." That was certainly saying something, since Moose had been six foot three and required a custom longboard to accommodate his 250-pound frame. But Grant knew his mom was right. She continued, "He hated it that Gator never seemed to get over Moose's choice to sell off his shares of the family property to move to Florida."

Grant pointed his finger in the air. "That's exactly what I told Rebekah."

"And Rebekah is the very beautiful and very smart director of Furever Paws that you keep flying to North Carolina to visit?" His mom's knowing smile lit up her face.

"I haven't been flying up there *just* to visit her," Grant said. He wanted to tell his mom about the babies. But he'd made a promise to wait a few more weeks. "How did you know about me and Rebekah, anyway?"

"Because there're only two things that would keep my son from work."

"Oh, yeah?" He lifted himself into a sitting position on the counter near the sink. "What are those?"

"Either a sweet set breaking off the south shore or a sweet someone needing him."

Grant rolled his shoulders. "How do you know that it's Rebekah that needs me?"

His mother studied him the way she used to when he'd been a kid and would promise to reapply his sunscreen, but then inevitably returned home with a sunburned face. "You're so much like your father, always the first one in line to help out with no thought as to what it might cost you in the long run. It kept me up a lot of nights when you volunteered for the lifeguarding deep sea rescue team. But you can't always save everyone, Grant."

"Who am I trying to save?" he asked. Rebekah certainly wasn't the kind of person who needed rescuing. She was far too strong, too controlled, to need anyone.

"Um, how about me, for one?" His mom gestured at the water stain on the ceiling. "You didn't have to rush here to deal with this, you know."

"You told me that there was a major leak at the surf shop."

"Yeah, but only because I wanted to know if your sister and I could store some of the merchandise at that fancy condo you hardly ever seem to use anymore. Not because I needed you to fly home and help me dump out buckets. And do you really think that Bunny and Birdie need you swinging by North Carolina every week or so to oversee the pet shelter that they've been running on their own for how many years?"

Okay, so his mom had a good point. He would've told her as much; however, she continued talking.

"Rushing in to rescue people is your way of having a little adventure. First you wanted to be a lifeguard. But then you saw that the surf shop had been hit by the recession, so you decided that a better-paying job would provide you with more income to send our way. The next step was getting into the business of saving companies by rebranding their products. Now you're this marketing genius who makes more money than you know what to do with, and yet you're still restless. Have you ever thought that maybe you need to take a step back and figure out what's missing in your *own* life that makes you want to become so involved in everyone else's?"

"Geez, Mom." Grant felt the weight of his mother's

knowing stare. "You make it sound like I'm a solution in search of a problem."

"Kiddo, how easily could you cut a check to Bunny and Birdie to get them back on their feet after that tornado?"

"You know they won't take money from me."

"Exactly. So you found other ways to help them. Whether they want that help or not."

"Of course they want my help. You should see how happy they are every time I come out."

His mom lifted her brows and he recognized her playful smirk because it was the same one he made when he was holding back his own laughter. "It just so happens that by helping them, you also get to help yourself to more time with their director."

There was a puddle of water on the counter next to him and he used his fingers to flick some her way. "Are you done teasing me now?"

His mom's squeal of laughter brought one of Grant's sisters to the doorway between the shop and the shaping room. "Some of us are trying to make phone calls to our vendors and order replacements for all the merchandise that got ruined last night. You think you guys could keep it down back here while you discuss Grant's new girlfriend?"

Clearly, his family had already heard about her, which meant the news of their fake relationship had already made its way down here.

"You know, I was going to help you clean up this mess and then buy you guys lunch." Grant said with a dismissive shrug. "But I wouldn't want to make myself too helpful."

His sister's reply was to stick her tongue out at him, making his mom laugh even harder.

After his conversation with his mom and then a question-fueled lunch with his little sister, Grant's head was swirling with thoughts of Rebekah. He found himself checking his phone for missed texts every fifteen minutes while he finished clearing wet debris and soggy cardboard boxes from the storage room of his family's surf shop.

He wasn't sure if he should give Rebekah space or if he should try to reach out and apologize for leaving so soon after promising to stick by her side.

They hadn't exactly parted on the best of terms. She'd brought up all that stuff about Gator, and then she'd cried in his arms about her previous pregnancy. The woman had finally let down her guard in front of him and he'd taken off.

Although, in his defense, he'd thought his mom actually needed him.

But Rebekah had needed him, too.

Or maybe not.

The sex had been incredible and at first, that had been enough of a reason to fly up to see her. But soon, he found that he couldn't stop thinking about her— and now that he had a chance at a real relationship and future with her, the fact that she might not want the same hurt more than he expected. There were too many emotions swirling around in his head and not a single clear thought. He stretched, and his eyes landed on his dad's old longboard hanging on the wall in the rear of the store. Moose Whitaker used to always say that the ocean washed away the world's problems.

Had there ever been a better time to hit the waves?

Rebekah didn't hear from Grant that entire Saturday. On Sunday evening, she got a text from him asking her how Angus was doing. But there was no reference to her pregnancy or her emotional breakdown in his rental car a couple of nights ago. In response, Rebekah sent a picture of Angus chomping away at his food bowl. Then asked, How are things going at your family's surf shop?

Grant wrote, It was a mess, but my mom has it under control.

Rebekah frowned at her screen. So, now that the leak situation had been taken care of, was he planning to return to Spring Forest anytime soon? To pick up where they'd left off?

Angus hopped up onto the sofa beside her, that stupid T-shirt of Grant's hanging from his little mouth. "I know you miss him, boy." She stroked the spiky hair that made the dog look as though he had serious eyebrows. "But who knows when he'll come back. He lives in Florida."

She sighed and leaned her head against the white leather, watching the rain falling outside her window. This would probably be the same conversation she'd be having with her kids a couple of years from now. *I know you miss Daddy, kids. But he has a life somewhere else. Who knows when we'll see him again?*

Just thinking about the hurt on her unborn children's

faces made Rebekah want to forget Grant's phone number all over again.

On Monday, she threw herself back into her job. Not that Rebekah didn't always fully commit to her work, but she'd made a promise to herself the previous night that she could only control what she did with her life. She couldn't control Grant.

Angus had a little bed in the corner of her office, but if she got up to get something out of a filing cabinet or to head to the reception desk to scan the latest adoption report, the dog trotted along behind her.

"All that time alone on the streets and now the little guy won't leave your side," Bunny said, bending down in her work overalls to give Angus one of the small treats she always carried in her pockets for the animals.

"I know." Rebekah's shoulders dropped. "Hopefully, it's a good family that eventually adopts him."

"Families don't always pick the animals they're going to adopt." Bunny rose to her feet and stared at her through clear blue eyes. "Sometimes, it's the animals who pick the families."

Grant had told her something similar, but she didn't want to hear it any more now than she had last week. Rebekah pivoted toward the reception desk, looking for some papers or folders or anything else that needed her attention so that she wouldn't have to face the older woman and pretend that she didn't know exactly what Bunny meant.

"How about all that rain we got yesterday?" Bunny said, thankfully changing the subject. "The storm also hit Florida pretty badly before coming up here to us."

Was the mention of Florida supposed to be an opening for bringing up Grant? If so, she wasn't going to fall for it. Rebekah managed a murmur as she arranged the clipboards holding blank adoption applications.

"I called Grant last night to tell him that we're having some drainage issues with the creek that runs through the farm." Yep, Bunny had purposely steered the conversation in the direction of her perfect nephew, the Whitaker golden boy.

Rebekah's spine straightened. "Let me guess. He's on his way to save the day?"

"That's the weird thing." The woman's head tilted so far to the side, the messy white bun on top was in danger of tumbling down. "Lately, he's come running at the slightest mention of a problem on the farm or with the shelter. But this time all he did was offer to call an excavation company to come out and take a look."

"Well, he might be pretty busy with his job in Jacksonville. He *has* been out of his office a lot lately."

"But that's because he has someone special now in Spring Forest."

"No, he comes to see you and Birdie, too."

Rebekah realized her slip as soon as the corner of Bunny's mouth lifted slightly. Damn. The woman had gotten her to admit that not only had she observed Grant's comings and goings, but also that she knew it had something to do with their relationship. The relationship that was supposed to only be pretend.

"Well, when you talk to him today, let him know that Megan Jennings is going to want to meet with all of us soon." Bunny gave Angus another treat before walking away.

If Megan—the lawyer investigating the Whitakers' financial problems—wanted to meet, that probably meant there had been a break in the case. Grant would want to know...but it wasn't as if Rebekah was going to bring up the subject of his aunts' missing money, let alone the findings of the attorney's investigation. Let Megan be the one to tell Grant that his Uncle Gator was clearly behind the whole thing.

When she left work that afternoon, Rebekah saw the yellow backhoe chugging along the creek on the farm's property. She half expected to see Grant in the driver's seat, trying to dig the new drainage trench himself. The guy came to town to take pictures for brochures or to take forty-five minute tours of bird sanctuaries that he'd already researched online. But suddenly he couldn't be bothered with a major problem like this?

It didn't make any sense.

Unless he was avoiding something in Spring Forest. Or someone.

Chapter Fourteen

This was the first time Grant had flown into Spring Forest and immediately hadn't gone by Furever Paws to see Rebekah.

Well, at least the first time since they initially slept together.

He drove his rental car to the Main Street Grille, where he was meeting his aunts and Megan Jennings.

When they'd called him earlier this week about the drainage issue on their creek, it had taken every ounce of strength to stop himself from coming running. But unless his aunts or Rebekah specifically said that they needed his help, he'd vowed not to rush in and rescue anyone again.

Then, last night, Birdie had told him that they needed to talk to him about their financial situation, and that was all it had taken to get him to hop on a plane.

"Hey, Whitaker," a voice said when Grant exited his car. He turned and saw one of his old buddies from his summer visits to his aunts.

"Zeke Harper." Grant smiled as he met the man halfway across the parking lot. They shared a handshake. "I'd heard you'd come back to town after getting out of the Army."

"I keep thinking I'll run into you over at the shelter one of these days." Zeke studied him with avid interest. The psychologist was involved with local veterans' groups and he and his fiancé had even started a therapy dog training program matching pets to soldiers with PTSD. "Mollie says you've been flying into Spring Forest quite a bit lately."

"I bet she says a lot of things to you now that you guys are finally engaged." Mollie McFadden and her brother had grown up with Zeke and, while Grant had usually only hung out with the older guys, he now saw Mollie holding training classes over at Furever Paws pretty regularly. "Took you two long enough, huh?"

"All good things are worth the wait," Zeke said, then lifted a single brow. "How's your own wait going?"

"Since you're a head doctor, should I even bother pretending that I don't know exactly who you're talking about?"

"Doesn't take a psychology degree to know that you've got a thing for Rebekah Taylor."

"Can I take that to mean that people are already talking?" Grant asked, wondering how much everyone knew. Did they realize she was pregnant?

"Spring Forest has grown a lot since we were kids,

but it's still a small town at heart. However, if you ever want to swing by my office in Raleigh for some relationship advice, I can invoke doctor/patient privilege, so you don't have to worry about the gossip."

"I just might take you up on that," Grant said as he spotted his aunts walking along the sidewalk with their attorney. "I've gotta go, but I'm sure we'll run into each other soon."

He and Zeke exchanged another handshake and Grant had just enough time to make it to the restaurant's entrance to hold the door open for the trio of women.

"Grant, you remember Megan Jennings," Aunt Birdie said. "She lives out at Battle Lands Farms with her boyfriend, Cade. I'm sure Rebekah's already told you how Megan and Cade have the best luck placing all the animals they foster."

"Of course." Grant shook the young woman's hand, not revealing that Rebekah hadn't told him anything of the sort. They'd barely been willing to discuss their own relationship, let alone anyone else's. "I hear you might have some news for us."

Megan exchanged a look with his aunts and Grant's stomach dropped. He had a feeling he wasn't going to like what he was about to hear.

"Let's get a table and we can talk about everything," Aunt Bunny suggested. "I've been craving a tuna melt and a chocolate shake all week."

They were seated at a booth in the corner, away from the other customers, and Grant realized that someone had called ahead to reserve this particular table. That meant his aunts wanted privacy, but they also planned to tell him something in a public place. Did they think he was going to get upset?

"Just lay it on me," he finally said when the server left with their order.

Birdie looked across the table to Bunny, who nodded. The older sister took a deep breath. "Megan came to us a while ago with some information and we've been going back and forth on what we should do with it."

Grant pinched the bridge of his nose, already knowing what they were going to say. "It was Gator, wasn't it?"

Megan began speaking. Apparently, his uncle had gotten himself into some serious financial trouble and dipped into his sisters' financial interests to cover his own bad debts.

"When Gator pocketed those insurance premiums, his embezzlement affected Furever Paws, which operates as a nonprofit organization. Bunny and Birdie have a fiduciary duty to protect their nonprofit's assets and provide their promised services. Grant, if your aunts don't file charges to get that money back, not only do they breach that duty, they also risk losing the trust of their donors. They could pretty much kiss all future grants and zoning approvals goodbye, as well. If they want to keep Furever Paws open, they have to bring a case against your uncle and at least attempt to recoup their losses."

Grant felt all the air leave his lungs as his whole childhood deflated. "Have you talked to Gator?"

"That's the thing," Birdie said. "Nobody's seen him since the investigation started."

"Before we formally file the charges, we wanted to talk to you and your cousins first," Bunny explained. "Wanted y'all to see why we have no choice."

"What do Gator's kids say about this?" Grant asked.

"Well, they aren't very happy with their father, obviously. They think he should turn himself in."

Grant stared at Megan. "Is there any way to prosecute my uncle without my aunts having to be the ones who point the finger? I just don't want Gator to think his family betrayed him."

Birdie shared the bench seat with Grant and he could feel her sit up straighter. "Gator betrayed us first by taking our money. We trusted him to manage our affairs and instead of making insurance payments, he covered his own behind, leaving us with no resources when the tornado struck. His deception got us into a mountain of debt that we'll probably never get out of as far as our personal finances. As far as the animal shelter goes, we're left with a shoestring budget based on charitable donations. But how long will those keep coming in? Especially if folks find out that we aren't doing right by their donations?"

Grant was the source of several large donations—anonymously, of course—but the shelter needed the support of the whole community.

"If your aunts hope to recoup any of their lost money," Megan explained, "then they need to press charges. Otherwise, the insurance company won't reimburse them because there would be no evidence of a crime committed."

"I'm hearing everything you guys are saying." Grant

let out another rush of air through his nostrils. "And from a legal standpoint, it makes perfect sense. But I'm just having a hard time wrapping my head around the fact that Uncle Gator could do something like this. Growing up, he constantly preached to me about taking care of family. What about all those comments he used to make about my dad ditching his family to move to Florida?"

"I never really understood why he was so sore about that," Bunny said, shaking her head. "By moving to Florida, Moose *was* taking care of his family. His new family that he was creating. That's where your mom lived and she was already pregnant with you. It's not like he abandoned Whitaker Acres or anything. Moose sent you kids to us every summer so that you'd love the land as much as we do."

Their lunch arrived, but Grant had a difficult time swallowing his food. He only made it halfway through before his fingers began twitching. He rose to his feet and pulled his wallet out of his pocket. "I really should be heading back."

He dropped some bills on the table, then promised his aunts that he'd be back in town soon and kissed each of them on their weathered cheeks.

He didn't feel much like driving back to the airport in Raleigh–Durham, though, so he decided to walk around downtown Spring Forest for a bit.

His thoughts were so consumed with the weight of accepting Gator's involvement in embezzling from his aunts that he didn't quite know how long he'd been wandering around until he found himself standing in front of the abandoned house on Second Avenue. The one he and Rebekah had followed Angus to.

As he stood in front of the overgrown yard, Aunt Bunny's words kept replaying in his head. His father had left Spring Forest because he was expecting a new family.

Could Grant make the same sacrifice?

So Grant had been in town yesterday and hadn't sent her so much as a text, let alone stopped in to the shelter and said hello. Rebekah looked at Angus, who was now sitting in the front passenger seat of her car as she drove to work the following morning.

If the guy wanted to avoid her, that was one thing. But why hadn't he wanted to see Angus? Back at the townhome, the dog had dragged that stupid T-shirt out the front door with him this morning and Rebekah had had to wrestle it away before they got out of the car in the Furever Paws parking lot.

Rebekah should've known by the way Angus's ears perked up that something was going on besides a simple game of tug-of-war. But it wasn't until she was opening the passenger door for the dog that she realized the person getting out of the blue SUV next to her was Grant. Angus dashed out of the door before she could clip his leash on him. Her heart slammed into her chest and she sucked air into her lungs before yelling, "Angus, come back!"

But instead of taking off, the dog danced around Grant's feet, yipping and barking and wagging his tail.

"Did you miss me, boy? Huh? Did you?" Grant knelt

down to pet Angus, who immediately rolled onto his back and exposed his belly. "You missed Daddy."

Rebekah wanted to shout that he wasn't anyone's daddy. At least, not yet. But she held herself back and instead jerked her chin toward his full-size SUV. "Did they give you a free upgrade at the rental counter?"

"Oh, that's not a rental car. I drove up from Jacksonville…" Before he could finish, another vehicle pulled into the lot so quickly it kicked up gravel behind its tires. "Can you excuse me for a second?"

She recognized the person behind the wheel as Gator Whitaker and Rebekah's heartbeat picked up speed. Nobody had seen the man for a while, so if he was showing up now, something big was going on. Grant hadn't wanted to believe anything bad about his uncle the last time Rebekah brought up the subject. Had anything changed since Grant's meeting with the aunts and Megan Jennings yesterday?

"Thanks for agreeing to talk," he said to his uncle through the open truck window.

Of course Grant hadn't actually come to see Rebekah. He was here to meet with his family, to probably plead his uncle's case and get his aunts not to press charges. Judging by the idling engine, Gator had no intention of coming inside. She could only make out a few words of what the man was saying to his nephew, but his face was red and his hands were gesturing wildly.

"Come on, Angus." She scooped up the dog in her arms. Neither one of them needed to be a witness to the family drama unfolding out here.

When she got to the building's entrance, Bunny and

Birdie were already coming outside and their attorney was behind them. Despite the emotionally charged situation occurring in the parking lot, the older women still managed to say hello to Angus as they walked toward the idling truck.

"Let's move over here," Megan said to Rebekah.

"Actually, I was heading inside," Rebekah told the woman who had her smartphone out and was discreetly aiming it at Gator's truck.

"The police have already been called and are on their way," Megan whispered. "But it would help to have plenty of witnesses out here, just in case Gator admits anything."

Rebekah didn't want to be a witness. And she especially didn't want to hear Grant stick up for his uncle again. But she reluctantly let Megan lead her closer so they could hear the heated conversation.

The voices grew louder and Rebekah shifted from one foot to the other, wishing she'd just let Angus keep the T-shirt when they first arrived. She would've already been inside the building when Grant had pulled up and someone else could've been a witness.

"Now, Gator, you've left us with no choice," Bunny said. "If we want to recoup our money and protect our fiduciary duty, we have to press charges."

"This is the thanks I get?" she heard Gator yell at his sisters. "Neither one of you could find husbands of your own, and I was the only one who stuck by you two when everyone else in the family deserted you."

Rebekah's indrawn breath made Angus squirm in her arms. "Shhh. It's okay. Hold still."

She wished she hadn't dropped his leash when he'd darted out of the car. There was no way she was going to walk all the way back there now to get it and draw any more attention to herself or Megan, who was still recording the argument.

"That was a low blow," Grant warned his uncle, and Rebekah was relieved to hear him defend the older women. Bunny had been engaged when she was younger and still spoke fondly of her fiancé, who'd died tragically. Birdie...well, Rebekah wasn't sure if Birdie had ever been married or in any type of romantic relationship because nobody had ever said one way or the other.

"We didn't *need* you to take care of things for us." Birdie crossed her arms over the front of her work shirt. "You insisted that you could double our investments. I believe your exact words were, *I want you gals to focus on your animal shelter. I'll handle the bills*. But you handled that money straight into your own pocket, Gator."

"You think I wasn't planning to pay you guys back?" Gator pounded his steering wheel. "I kept track of every single penny I borrowed. But I'm telling you right now that if you don't drop these charges, you'll never see that money again."

"Bingo," Megan whispered.

Grant stepped in front of Birdie and was only inches away from the truck window. "Gator, if you ever threaten my aunts again..."

Rebekah could see Grant's lips moving, but the approaching sirens drowned out his words. Gator's response was equally muted but the beefy fist raised in his nephew's direction left little doubt as to what was going to happen next.

Angus gave a fierce bark and leaped out of Rebekah's arms, tearing across the parking lot in Grant's direction. She ran after him, but the truck tires were already spinning and it felt as though everything after that happened in slow motion.

Rebekah didn't hear the roar of the engine or the wail of the sirens or the cries of the Whitaker sisters. The only sound was the blood pounding in her ears as she raced toward Angus.

But she was too late. The poor gray dog bounced off the front wheel as Gator accelerated out of the parking lot.

Chapter Fifteen

"Have you heard anything?" Grant tried to keep his voice low as he slipped into the small room outside of the veterinarian's surgery.

Rebekah's eyes were puffy and her cheeks were still stained with tears when she lifted her head. "Not really. Lauren didn't think that his legs were broken, but, oh, Grant, there was so much blood all over his little head."

"I know, sweetheart." Grant lowered himself into the chair beside her and pulled her into his side, stroking her back as she shuddered several times. "But Angus is our Scottish warrior, remember. He's tough. He's going to get through this."

"He was trying to protect you," Rebekah said before sniffing. "When it looked like Gator was going to punch you, that's when he took off running. He thought he could save you."

Grant's head fell back against the wall and he pulled Rebekah tighter to him. "I'm so sorry, Rebekah. I should've known that I couldn't talk any sense into my uncle. I thought that I could reason with him and that he'd simply turn himself in to the authorities. Instead, I put you and Angus and even my aunts in a horrible situation. I didn't expect him to be that angry. That hostile."

"That's who you are, Grant." She lifted her face to his. "You always expect the best from people. And I always expect the worst."

"Well, in this particular situation, you were right. I should've listened to you."

"So what happened with your uncle? Did the cops ever catch up to him?"

"I'm sure they will." He shrugged.

Rebekah stiffened against him as she sat up straighter. "Why aren't you out there searching for him?"

He pushed the hair back from her face and kissed her softly on the forehead. "Because you and Angus are the ones who need me right now."

Two hours later, Dr. Lauren came into the waiting area, pulling a surgical mask off her face. "Unfortunately, the left eyeball was completely perforated by the impact and we had to remove it. I'm going to send him home with some pain meds and a list of concussion protocols I want you to follow."

"You're sending him home? With me?" Relief washed through Rebekah. "You mean he's going to be okay?"

Lauren nodded. "It's going to take him a while to adjust to having just one eye. So his balance and his steering, so to speak, might be a little off at first. You'll have to apply an ointment on the area to keep it infection free and I'll need to see him again in about a week to remove the sutures."

Rebekah stood up and threw her arms around the veterinarian, who returned the hug. It wasn't Rebekah's most professional moment, but she wasn't here as a professional. She was here as a mom.

Grant rose to his feet and extended his hand. "Thank you so much, Doc."

"Oh!" Rebekah turned to the tote bag under her chair and pulled out a scrap of cotton. "Could you put this beside him so that when he wakes up, he has it with him?"

"Was that my favorite T-shirt?" Grant asked when Lauren returned to the surgical area.

"Yeah. You left it at my house. Angus found it under the bed and has been carrying it around with him everywhere."

"Poor guy missed me that much, huh?"

"He didn't know if you were going to come back." Rebekah instinctively lowered her eyes, but then she caught herself. No. It was time to have an honest conversation with the man, once and for all. She lifted her face to his. "Actually, Grant, neither one of us knew if you were coming back."

"Of course I was planning to come back. I told you that I was committed to being a father to the twins."

"But you're always on the go and I don't want our

children growing up never knowing when they'll see you again."

"I'll see them as often as you'll let me. Rebekah, I've tried like hell to give you space, to let you come to your own conclusions about the kind of guy I am."

"Is that why you didn't come see me the last time you were in town? You were trying to give me space?"

"Well, recently it was pointed out to me that I have a tendency to rush in to help people who don't always need my help."

"I don't know what I need yet, Grant. But I don't want to start depending on you if you're going to fly off anytime it suits you."

"Sweetheart, you have no idea how much I hate planes. I would gladly give up my frequent flyer card if it means you're finally willing to let me be a part of our children's lives."

When he called her sweetheart and made promises like that, Rebekah's head fought to keep her emotions in check. And the thing her head kept telling her was that he'd only committed to being a part of their children's lives, not hers. Sure, as their mother, he couldn't very well be active in their lives and not hers. But he'd yet to say anything about being a boyfriend, let alone a husband. Not that she'd given him the opportunity to do so.

Davis, the vet tech, opened the door, causing Rebekah to jump back from Grant's embrace. "He's starting to come out of the anesthesia if y'all want to step on back."

Rebekah cleared her throat and rose to her feet.

"Hey," Grant said, slipping his hand into hers as he

followed her into the operating room. "I'm not leaving town again until we finish this conversation."

It turned out that Grant didn't get on a plane again. At least, not that week. Or the one after.

But they only spoke about the babies in terms of the immediate future. They didn't commit to any sort of long-term plan.

As if by unspoken agreement, he stayed at Rebekah's place with her and Angus, who was not very happy about having to wear the protective cone of shame to keep him from using his front paws to scratch at the healing incision where his eye used to be.

Rebekah went into the office during the days and Grant stayed home with the dog, setting up a command post on her kitchen table with his laptop, tablet and smartphone. He sent emails, walked the dog, attended video conferences, applied the antibiotic ointment the vet recommended, studied marketing trend reports and used his Bluetooth headset to make phone calls while simultaneously doing the online grocery shopping.

And then he slept in Rebekah's bed with her at night.

"You know, I could get pretty used to this stay-at-home dad life," he said, stretching in her bed as he watched her get dressed for work the following Friday morning.

"I'd like to hear that again in seven months when it's a dog *and* two babies." Rebekah's smile revealed her two adorable dimples. But her face soon turned down into a frown when she tried to zip up her dress.

"Here, let me help you," he said, getting up out of bed.

"Ugh." She dropped her arms in defeat. "I think I'm

going to need to start investing in maternity clothes pretty soon. I don't know how much longer I can hide it."

"If it were up to me, you wouldn't be hiding it all," he reminded her, slipping his arms around her waist and resting his hands over the still small bump under her midsection.

She leaned her head back onto his shoulder and sighed. "I have that appointment with Dr. Singh next week. Maybe we can start telling people after that."

"Good. Because I'm ready to stop sneaking around." He felt her stiffen, but he wasn't sure if it was in response to his words, or to the sudden ringing of her cell phone on the bedside table.

He watched her walk across the room to retrieve it, her smooth skin exposed from the unzipped back of her dress.

"It's for you," she said a few moments later, handing him her device. "Apparently everyone knows where to find you when you don't answer your own phone."

Which was exactly why he thought they should no longer be referring to their relationship as pretend. Everyone knew he'd been staying here and that something had been going on between them for a while. And there was certainly no faking the attraction.

"Hello," he said, then listened to Birdie's rapid-fire questions about the cell tower contract he'd sent his aunts last night to peruse. Rebekah had already laid the groundwork with the city council to get the zoning approved. But now the contract needed to be negotiated. With Gator's recent arrest and vows to fight them in court, his aunts were eager to have more income.

"Yes, the tower company would have full rights to that half acre of land, but you can stipulate in the contract that you get a percentage of any money they make from any secondary service providers. If you go through an agency that represents landowners, they can negotiate the best deal on your behalf."

He answered a few more questions and then disconnected. Rebekah was still standing there, although she'd put on a looser dress that showed her rounded shoulders.

He leaned his elbows back on the bed and appreciated the view. "Well, my aunt needs someone to fly to D.C. to meet with the agency that will negotiate the contract for the cell tower."

"So, when do you leave?" Rebekah asked.

"That's the thing. You're going to have to go instead. Dr. Singh didn't say anything about you not being allowed to fly, right?"

"Why would I go? I only manage the business deals that have to do with the shelter, not the Whitaker property."

"Because I just found out that my Uncle Gator finally turned himself in and I want to be there to support my cousins when they attend his arraignment." He saw the sympathetic look in her eye and before she could tell him for the hundredth time how proud she was of him for defending his aunts, he added, "Plus, I promised to turn in my frequent flyer card, remember?"

"You don't really expect me to hold you to that, do you, Grant? Obviously, you're going to have to return to Florida eventually."

"Eventually," he agreed. "But not until I put all your doubts about me to rest."

* * *

Grant and Angus drove her to the airport and Rebekah was able to meet with the cell tower representatives, as well as the landowner agency, to work out the specifics for the deal that would give Whitaker Acres an added boost to their monthly income.

She'd been a little surprised that both he and his aunts trusted her to make the best deal for them after they'd recently been burned by an actual family member. Grant's confidence in her made her go into that negotiation with the desire to accept nothing less than top dollar for her bosses.

Just like he had this past week when Rebekah was gone for the day at work, Grant sent her pictures of Angus carrying around whichever discarded item of her clothing he'd been able to find that day. And with the amount of time that she and Grant had spent getting out of their clothes lately, it was usually whatever had ended up closest to the bed.

So that night, as she lay in the hotel room, the picture that came in was of the dog curled up on the white sofa with one of her favorite bras as his pillow. She made a mental note to get a laundry hamper with a lid.

It was weird to think that a little over a month ago she'd been living on her own, perfectly happy and comfortable in the quiet, organized world she'd created for herself. Yet now a man and a dog were taking up residence in her townhome and it almost felt normal.

The following day, after her plane landed, she missed the bottom step off the escalator because she was so surprised to see Grant standing in the baggage claim area, a bouquet of plumeria in one hand and Angus's leash in the other.

She immediately bent down and greeted Angus first. "What are you doing here, big guy? Did you miss me?"

"Well, we both missed you," Grant said, then shot Angus a playful look of chastisement. "But some of us know better than to yip and prance around and draw attention to ourselves in a public place."

"Nothing draws more attention than a bouquet of flowers and a cute dog," a familiar voice said behind Rebekah.

"What are you doing here, Aunt Birdie?" Grant asked the woman who had a bright pink carry-on case at her feet. Then he looked at the man behind his aunt. "And why did you ask Doc J to pick you up from the airport? I could've given you a ride."

Rebekah smiled at the appearance of the retired veterinarian, then bit back a giggle when she saw that he had his own small duffel clutched in one of his hands. The doctor knelt down to greet Angus. "I've heard all about you, my friend. Running all over town and causing quite the stir. But I see my daughter did a heck of a job sewing up that incision. We'll need to get you a little pirate patch to complete the look."

While the two older people were distracted fussing over the dog, Rebekah used her elbow to nudge Grant. When she finally got his attention, she nodded toward the boarding passes in Doc J's free hand.

"You mean…you guys are here together?" Grant's voice was loud enough to make Rebekah wince.

Doc J grinned sheepishly at Birdie. "Guess the cat's finally out of the bag."

"Oh, don't look so shocked, Grant. Richard has always been sweet on me. Now that he's retired and we no longer work together, I figure why not kick up my heels while I'm still young enough to kick 'em."

"So you two…" Grant pointed at his aunt's suitcase. "Are you moving down to Florida, too?"

"Not permanently. I just go down for the occasional weekend getaway with my man."

Her man, indeed! Rebekah wanted to give her boss a high five. There'd been rumors about Doc J having some sort of secret crush, but nobody had been able to figure out which Whitaker sister it was since he spent time with both of them.

This time, Rebekah got to be the one smiling at Grant's look of confusion instead of the other way around. He opened his mouth several times, only to close it again.

"But what about Bunny?" Grant finally got the words out.

"What about her?" Birdie put her hands on her hips.

"It's always been the two of you together," Grant said, then looked to Rebekah for confirmation. Nope, he wasn't getting any support from her. She remembered how he'd sat back in his chair at the barbecue restaurant, practically egging her parents on as they'd asked her all those embarrassing questions. "Isn't Bunny worried that a man might come between you?"

"Psh." Birdie waved a hand at him. "Bunny has been talking to her own gentleman online for the past five years."

At this, Rebekah really did give the older woman a high five. She wished Bunny could've been there and gotten one, as well.

"Did you know about this?" Grant tilted his head at Rebekah.

"I had no idea." Rebekah grinned. "And usually I know everything that's going on at Furever Paws."

"Well, you've been so busy keeping your own secrets—" Birdie glanced down at Rebekah's waistline "—you haven't had time to notice mine."

Heat flooded Rebekah's cheeks and her hands immediately shot to her stomach, which probably only confirmed his aunt's suspicions. Well, that and the fact that Grant shifted the flowers to the hand holding the leash and protectively slipped his free arm around her waist.

"Just for the record…" Grant cleared his throat. "We were planning to tell you guys about the pregnancy after the doctor's appointment next week."

Birdie winked at her nephew. "Good. This means you'll be in town more often and can help out with planning the Paws Under the Stars event."

"Paws Under the Stars?" Rebekah lifted her eyebrow.

"That's the name Grant came up with for our fundraiser gala. We both thought Fur Ball sounded too stuffy." Birdie's hands were clasped together in excitement. "Now, Richard and I have a plane to catch, so you two rest up this weekend and let me know what time our doctor's appointment is next week."

Rebekah's eyes widened in concern. There weren't enough chairs in the obstetrician's office for all the Whitakers.

Chapter Sixteen

The Paws Under the Stars event wasn't only a fund-raiser, it was also a huge celebration of the recent ad-ditions to the Furever Paws facility. Grant had never thought of himself as a party planner, but working with Rebekah handling the dinner, dance and silent auction, he'd never been more certain that he could easily work with her for the rest of their lives.

It had been a month since they'd run into his Aunt Birdie and Doc J at the airport, and Grant had only been back to Jacksonville once, to hand in his resigna-tion and to tell his mom and his sisters about his future plans. He hadn't moved in officially with Rebekah, but she and Angus also hadn't kicked him out of her place.

Uncle Gator had reluctantly agreed to a plea deal earlier this week and yesterday's ultrasound at the doctor's revealed that he and Rebekah were having a boy and a girl. They had so much to celebrate, Grant was determined to make tonight's gala the party of the year.

He drove Angus to the animal shelter later that morning and, when he walked into Rebekah's office, he handed her the chocolate croissant and decaf latte she'd sworn off yesterday after getting on the scale at Dr. Singh's office. If you asked Grant, though, Rebekah's new pregnancy curves made her look even sexier.

"Looks like the white tents are being set up now," he said after kissing her cheek. "Angus and I are going to take a walk and make sure they get those little twinkly lights up in all the trees."

"Grant, are you sure we needed to rent tents? I keep crunching the numbers and, at this rate, our only profit is going to be from the silent auction donations."

"Well, we sold way more tickets than even I expected and the newly built party pavilion—which was a brilliant decision on my part, by the way—isn't going to be big enough to hold everyone."

"Fine," she sighed, then bit into her still-warm croissant, pleasure written all over her face. It was the same expression he'd left her with this morning in bed after he'd—

"I trust you know what you're doing," she said around a mouthful of pastry.

Grant's lungs stopped working for a full fifteen seconds. While they'd been practically living together for the past month and she'd slowly been opening up to him more every day, having Rebekah finally say that she trusted him left him completely speechless.

When they walked outside, he looked down at Angus. "Did you hear that, boy? Mommy trusts me."

Angus replied with a yip.

"That's right." He scratched the dog's ears. "Tonight is definitely going to be a time for celebrations."

"Amanda, the food tastes fabulous," Rebekah told her friend, who still made time to walk dogs at the shelter despite having a new relationship and a new catering business.

"That's because all the fresh produce came from Battle Lands Farms," Amanda replied, having to raise her voice over the sound of the band that had just invited everyone out to the dance floor.

"Is Ryan around?" Rebekah scanned the formally dressed partygoers as they began dancing to a rendition of Elvis Presley's "Hound Dog." "I wanted to thank him for giving us that front page feature in *The Spring Forest Chronicle*."

"He's over there with Dillon and Tucker." Amanda pointed to where her boyfriend was standing with his son and their pet, a Chihuahua/dachshund mix. The boy and dog were wearing matching polka-dot bow ties.

Rebekah noticed the woman's hand immediately drop to her waist. It was the same motion Rebekah made whenever she felt one of the twins kicking. "Amanda, are you...?"

She let her question hang in the air, but her friend smiled as she gave a slow nod. "Ryan and I eloped last month. Tonight, Dillon has been walking around telling everyone that he and Tucker are going to be big brothers."

"Rebekah, can I borrow you for a sec?" Grant said in her ear as his hand slid over her elbow. Then he smiled at Amanda and added, "The food looks amazing, by the way."

"So do you two," Amanda said, giving Rebekah a subtle wink before waving goodbye. Amanda had been one of the women at happy hour with her the night she'd gone home with Grant. Rebekah slowly realized that Mollie and Claire, who'd also been there, probably had known about her and Grant the whole time.

When they were alone, Grant kissed her temple before whispering in her ear. "Aunt Bunny and Aunt Birdie were hoping that one of us would make some sort of speech thanking everyone for coming out tonight and supporting the shelter."

"But I didn't prepare a speech."

"Don't worry." Grant grinned. "I have us covered. Just come stand on the stage next to me."

Rebekah could feel the crowd's eyes on them as Grant held her hand, leading her to the raised dais inside the party pavilion. She tried to stand behind him as he took the microphone from the bandleader, who'd just finished singing Blake Shelton's "Ol' Red," another song about a dog. She was sensing a theme with the music selection.

"Thank you all for coming to Paws Under the Stars tonight and for supporting my aunts and all these wonderful animals," Grant started and the audience applauded.

"Many of you know Rebekah Taylor, the director of Furever Paws," he said, trying to urge her out from behind him. Embarrassment flooded her and she could only manage a small wave as the guests applauded again. "But what you might not know is that Rebekah had never had a pet before. And yet, just like many of you, she now has her own success story with fostering a dog."

It was then that Rebekah saw Lana Whitaker, Grant's mom—who she'd met earlier that afternoon—standing next to Rebekah's own parents at the side of the stage. Sheila held Angus's leash and walked the dog to greet them. Her dad stayed a few feet behind and let out a hearty sneeze.

"This is Angus," Grant continued. "His owner died and he'd been left to wander the streets of Spring Forest, evading capture for quite a while. But Rebekah spent time talking to Angus and leaving little treats for him. She eventually got him trust her and, well, Angus has a little gift he'd like to give his new mom to thank her for being so patient with both him *and* his new dad."

Rebekah's throat constricted and she forced herself to swallow her emotions.

"What's going on?" she whispered to Grant.

"This would've worked better if he hadn't refused to wear the kilt costume I got him for tonight," Grant announced into the microphone. Then he whispered to Rebekah, "Check out his plaid collar."

Rebekah's knees wobbled as she unsteadily knelt beside the dog. Hanging on a little silver loop near the buckle was a very large, very beautiful diamond ring.

She gasped and jerked her face up to look at Grant, only to find him on one knee beside her.

"I love you, Rebekah Taylor. I can't wait to be a father to our twins," he said, and a ripple of murmurs came from the dance floor. "But more than anything, I can't wait to be your husband. If you'll have me."

Rebekah's heart threatened to beat out of her chest. "Of course I'll have you, Grant Whitaker."

The crowd erupted in a cheer and Angus let out several yips and wiggled his tail as Grant tried to free the ring from the loop on his collar. When he finally slipped it onto Rebekah's finger, she lowered her voice and asked, "But what about your job?"

He handed the microphone back to the bandleader. "I gave them my resignation. I've already been hired for my first consulting job and I have it on good authority..." he jerked his chin toward Rebekah's father "...that plenty of men are now working from home and raising their kids."

All the blood rushed to her head, or maybe to her heart, and she got a fuzzy feeling of excitement. "You mean, you're going to move to Spring Forest?"

He squeezed her hand in his. "Look down at Angus's collar again."

There was a second loop that had been blocked by the leash clip. When Rebekah saw what was hanging there, her eyebrows slammed together. "Why are you giving me a key?"

"It's the key to that old brick house on Second Avenue," he explained, and Angus put his front paws on

Rebekah's thighs, causing her to sink from a kneeling position straight onto her rear end.

"You bought me that house?" If Rebekah hadn't already melted into a puddle of happiness, she certainly would have at his thoughtful and surprising gift.

"Well, I bought it mostly for Angus, but also for us. And the twins. I figure we're going to need that big yard for them to run in while I'm working from those patio benches you already have picked out in your mind."

"But what about your surfing?" She couldn't believe that he was giving up so much to be with her. How had she ever doubted him?

"We'll have to take lots of trips to the Outer Banks. In fact, my mom already brought Angus a custom life vest."

"Oh, Grant," she said, awkwardly trying to stand up. He held out his hand and pulled her to her feet. As soon as she was off the ground, she flung her arms around his neck. "I love you so much."

"You have no idea how long I've been waiting to hear that." He squeezed her to him and Angus let out another yip. Holding Rebekah with one arm, Grant bent down to lift up the dog to join them.

"Apparently, your aunt was right," Rebekah said around Angus's eager licks as the pup took turns kissing both of their faces.

"Right about what?" Grant asked, dodging a little pink tongue.

Rebekah's gaze swept across the gala guests lining up their animals for the much-anticipated pet parade, taking in all the familiar faces she'd met since moving to Spring Forest.

Her eyes returned to Grant's and she couldn't stop smiling. "It's amazing how much love your heart can accommodate once you decide to open it up."

* * * * *

Catch up with the previous stories in the
Furever Yours series

Look for
The Nanny Clause
by USA TODAY bestselling author
Karen Rose Smith
and The City Girl's Homecoming
by Kathy Douglass

Available now, wherever Harlequin Special Edition
books and ebooks are sold.

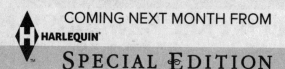

COMING NEXT MONTH FROM

HARLEQUIN®

SPECIAL EDITION

Available June 18, 2019

#2701 HER FAVORITE MAVERICK
Montana Mavericks: Six Brides for Six Brothers • by Christine Rimmer
Logan Crawford might just be the perfect man. A girl would have to be a fool to
turn him down. Or a coward. Sarah Turner thinks she might be both. But the single
mom has no time for love. Logan, however, is determined to steal her heart!

#2702 A PROMISE FOR THE TWINS
The Wyoming Multiples • by Melissa Senate
Former soldier Nick Garroway is in Wedlock Creek to fulfill a promise made to a
fallen soldier: check in on the woman the man had left pregnant with twins.
Brooke Timber is in need of a nanny, so what else can Nick do but fill in? She's also
planning her father's wedding, and all the family togetherness soon has Brooke
and Nick rethinking if this promise is still temporary.

#2703 THE FAMILY HE DIDN'T EXPECT
The Stone Gap Inn • by Shirley Jump
Dylan Millwright's bittersweet homecoming gets a whole lot sweeter when he
meets Abby Cooper. But this mother of two is all about "the ties that bind," and
Dylan isn't looking for strings to keep him down. But do this bachelor's wandering
ways conceal the secretly yearning heart of a family man?

#2704 THE DATING ARRANGEMENT
Something True • by Kerri Carpenter
Is the bride who fell on top of bar owner Jack Wright a sign from above? But event
planner Emerson Dewitt isn't actually a bride—much to her mother's perpetual
disappointment. Until Jack proposes an arrangement. He'll pose as Emerson's
boyfriend in exchange for her help relaunching his business. It's a perfect
partnership. Until all that fake dating turns into very real feelings...

#2705 A FATHER FOR HER CHILD
Sutter Creek, Montana • by Laurel Greer
Widow Cadence Grigg is slowly putting her life back together—and raising her
infant son. By her side is her late husband's best friend, Zach Cardenas, who can't
help her burgeoning feelings for Cadie and her baby boy. Though determined
not to fall in love again, Cadie might find that Cupid has other plans for her
happily-ever-after...

#2706 MORE THAN ONE NIGHT
Wildfire Ridge • by Heatherly Bell
A one-night stand so incredible, Jill Davis can't forget. Memories so delectable,
they sustained Sam Hawker through his final tour. Three years later, Jill is
unexpectedly face-to-face with her legendary marine lover. And it's clear their
chemistry is like gas and a match. Except Sam is her newest employee. That
means hands off, sister! Except maybe...just this once? Ooh-rah!

**YOU CAN FIND MORE INFORMATION ON UPCOMING HARLEQUIN® TITLES,
FREE EXCERPTS AND MORE AT WWW.HARLEQUIN.COM.**

HSECNM0619

Get 4 FREE REWARDS!

We'll send you 2 FREE Books
plus 2 FREE Mystery Gifts.

Harlequin® Special Edition books feature heroines finding the balance between their work life and personal life on the way to finding true love.

FREE
Value Over
$20

*Former soldier Nick Garroway is in Wedlock Creek
to fulfill a promise made to a fallen soldier: check in
on the woman the man had left pregnant with twins.
Brooke Timber is in need of a nanny, so what else can
Nick do but fill in? She's planning his father's wedding,
and all the family togetherness soon has Brooke and
Nick rethinking if this promise is still temporary…*

Read on for a sneak preview of
A Promise for the Twins,
*the next great book in Melissa Senate's
The Wyoming Multiples miniseries.*

If the Satler triplets were a definite, adding this client for July
would mean she could take off the first couple weeks of August,
which were always slow for Dream Weddings, and just be with
her twins.

Which would mean needing Nick Garroway as her nanny—
manny—until her regular nanny returned. Leanna could take some
time off herself and start mid-August. Win-win for everyone.

A temporary manny. A necessary temporary manny.

"Well, I've consulted with myself," Brooke said as she put
the phone on the table. "The job is yours. I'll only need help until
August 1. Then I'll take some time off, and Leanna, my regular
nanny, will be ready to come back to work for me."

He nodded. "Sounds good. Oh—and I know your ad called
for hours of nine to one during the week, but I'll make you a
deal. I'll be your around-the-clock nanny, as needed—for room
and board."

She swallowed. "You mean live here?"

"Temporarily. I'd rather not stay with my family. Besides, this way, you can work when you need to, not be boxed into someone else's hours."

Even a part-time nanny was very expensive—more than she could afford—but Brooke had always been grateful that necessity would make her limit her work so that she could spend real time with her babies. Now she'd have as-needed care for the twins without spending a penny.

Once again, she wondered where Nick Garroway had come from. He was like a miracle—and everything Brooke needed right now.

"I think I'm getting the better deal," she said. "But my grandmother always said not to look a gift horse in the mouth." Especially when that gift horse was clearly a workhorse.

"Good. You get what you need and I make good on that promise. Works for both of us."

She glanced at him. He might be gorgeous and sexy, and too capable with a diaper and a stack of dirty dishes, but he wasn't her fantasy in the flesh. He was here because he'd promised her babies' father he'd make sure she and the twins were all right. She had to stop thinking of him as a man—somehow, despite how attracted she was to him on a few different levels. He was her nanny, her *manny*.

But what was sexier than a man saying, "Take a break, I'll handle it. Take that call, I've got the kids. Go rest, I'll load the dishwasher and fold the laundry"?

Nothing was sexier. Which meant Brooke would have to be on guard 24/7.

Because her brain had caught up with her—the hot manny was moving into her house."

Don't miss
A Promise for the Twins *by Melissa Senate,*
available July 2019 wherever
Harlequin® *Special Edition books and ebooks are sold.*

www.Harlequin.com

HSEEXP0619

Looking for more satisfying love stories
with community and family at their core?

Check out **Harlequin® Special Edition**
and **Love Inspired®** books!

New books available every month!

CONNECT WITH US AT:

Facebook.com/groups/HarlequinConnection

 Facebook.com/HarlequinBooks

 Twitter.com/HarlequinBooks

 Instagram.com/HarlequinBooks

 Pinterest.com/HarlequinBooks

ReaderService.com

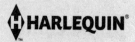

**ROMANCE WHEN
YOU NEED IT**

HFGENRE2018

Love Harlequin romance?

DISCOVER.

Be the first to find out about promotions, news and exclusive content!

 Facebook.com/HarlequinBooks

 Twitter.com/HarlequinBooks

 Instagram.com/HarlequinBooks

 Pinterest.com/HarlequinBooks

ReaderService.com

EXPLORE.

Sign up for the Harlequin e-newsletter and download a free book from any series at **TryHarlequin.com.**

CONNECT.

Join our Harlequin community to share your thoughts and connect with other romance readers!
Facebook.com/groups/HarlequinConnection

HARLEQUIN®

**ROMANCE WHEN
YOU NEED IT**

HSOCIAL2018